Dust Raising

SCEPTRE

Also by Christopher Burns

About the Body
Snakewrist
The Flint Bed
The Condition of Ice
In the Houses of the West

Dust Raising

CHRISTOPHER BURNS

SCEPTRE

First published in 1996 by Hodder and Stoughton
A division of Hodder Headline PLC
A Sceptre book

10 9 8 7 6 5 4 3 2 1

British Library Cataloguing in Publication Data

Burns, Christopher, 1944–
Dust Raising
1. English fiction – 20th century
I. Title
823.9'14 [F]

ISBN 0 340 66595 5

Typeset by Palimpsest Book Production Limited,
Polmont, Stirlingshire
Printed and bound in Great Britain by
Mackays of Chatham PLC, Chatham, Kent

Hodder and Stoughton
A division of Hodder Headline PLC
338 Euston Road
London NW1 3BH

For Paul and Judy

1

When I was a young man I had little discipline and less luck, and I justified my actions by telling myself that the only responsibility I had was to my work.

Things happened. They were a small part of my life and within a few months nothing remained of them. I disposed of evidence, destroyed photographs, deliberately lost contact with friends, and began to call myself by my middle name, not my first. I had always been known as Mick; now I only answered to Jamie.

After less than a year my real past had been isolated, contained, sealed, stored like a bacillus; only I knew that it had existed. In its place I invented a clearer, steadier past, and after a while I began to believe in my own invention. When required I could be nostalgic about a part of my life that never existed. No one recognised my lies, not even the woman I had been married to for over twenty years.

But sometimes my new life listed like a damaged vessel, its holds flooding with the realisation of what I had done in those far-off days, and I felt like a man clutching a guardrail as he is rolled inexorably towards black waves of humiliation and shame. Sometimes this sense of loss and guilt came upon me unexpectedly, often when I was with Lillian, and especially when I was with Claire. A chance remark or the appearance of a young woman, a total stranger, would shoulder me into vivid memory and speculation. I would sit darkly among the anecdotes and jokes until my silence was noted, and then I would apologise, laugh, and pretend that I was brooding about my next commission.

I was interviewed by a newspaper reporter who was writing a profile of me. I have had wide experience of such interviews, and I was happy with what I had said about my work and my past, but for the first time in half a lifetime I quoted my full name. That night a demon of conscience sank its claws into my dreams until I woke with a dizzying start.

The night was quiet; Lillian was asleep beside me; a photograph of our adopted daughter Claire stood on the bedside table; the digital clock kept its silent count. The house was secure, warm, as familiar and comforting as a shell.

And yet for several minutes, perhaps longer, it seemed to me that I was nothing but an actor, a man assuming a false identity written for him by a playful and vindictive god. Soon everything would be stripped away, and once the bright masque was finished, its colours faded to ash, I would be exiled among the remains of the life I had lived a quarter of a century ago. And this time I would know neither indifference nor hope. This time I would be condemned.

The morning's mail tumbled through the letterbox and fanned out like cards held in a gambler's hand.

Lillian picked up the white envelopes and extracted a glossy postcard from among them. It was from Claire. On the picture side was a photograph of the Mount Palomar observatory, and on the reverse was written *Another famous landmark!* Before she had gone to her American university

Claire joked that we talked too much about that country's cities and landscapes. Now she regularly sent us cards from some of the most photogenic examples. Lillian pinned them around the year planner on the display board, but we were running out of space. An earlier card of the Serpent Mound State Memorial in Ohio already obscured the end of December.

'Only one for me,' Lillian said, looking through the rest of the mail, 'the others are all for you. Including one marked Personal that's been passed on. It's nice, even handwriting – a woman's, I would guess.'

I glanced at the envelope which Lillian had placed on top of the others. It had been forwarded unopened by the newspaper which had published a profile of me three weeks ago. The sender had laid lengths of transparent tape across the flap like sticking-plaster.

Another plea, I thought: another student demanding help with their thesis, another artist consumed by a hopeless dream of fame, another crank who believes we share the same insights. I often received approaches such as this. They were always the last to be read and the last to be answered, if I bothered to respond at all. I put the letter to one side and began opening the others.

'I'm invited to a conference,' Lillian announced, and walked across the room to study the markers on the planner.

'For a day?'

'A whole week. Apparently curriculum design and development requires four and a half working days. It'll take me that long to read the back-up material.'

'When do you go?'

'The end of next month. I'll confirm it if it's all right by you. According to this, you'll still be here.'

'I imagine so. I don't intend to travel until the estate project is under way.'

'Good,' she said, looking up at the clock. 'Time's getting on. I really should be leaving, and so should you. Anything important?'

'Newsletters. Two investment statements; the results are good enough. An invitation to a private view that I'm not interested in attending. A catalogue of power tools, sculptors for the use of. And a request from the Tetmajer Gallery. If I'm able to suggest the name of a contemporary new traditionalist, they'd be grateful.'

'Can you?'

'I don't even know what a new traditionalist is. It sounds like a cynical marketing ploy. I suppose they've lost the courage of their convictions.'

'Edgar Tetmajer helped get you started. Maybe you should help him if you can.'

'I don't know the kind of artist his gallery wants. And I would have got started, as you put it, with or without Edgar Tetmajer.'

Nevertheless I read through the request again. The gallery was soliciting backing and creative input for a planned exhibition of figurative paintings, landscapes, still lives.

Almost twenty-five years ago, when I was little known and before I had started to work in chosen locations, the Tetmajer had shown some of my smaller pieces in an exhibition of new sculpture and installations. They had been sold at prices which I thought extravagant. A year later I decided that they had been underpriced, and that I had been badly advised. Of the six artists represented, four went on to secure international reputations. I was the best known of them all. I had had little to do with the gallery ever since.

Now it seemed that the Tetmajer had ceased to be adventurous. It had changed direction, in a mercenary appeal to conservatives and reactionaries who believed that painting ended with Degas and sculpture ended with Rodin.

I crumpled the appeal into a ball, lobbed it into a wastepaper basket, and held up a different letter.

'This is much more important. Ken Takama says that his team could clear the site within six weeks if I confirm a starting date. It takes that long to organise the heavy machinery.'

'But you haven't got a date.'

'Not yet. I'm still thinking about the topography of the place. I'm going to have another look at the wood today. And I want to make sure Ken can get me the aerial photographs that he promised. There shouldn't be any problem; the company has its own helicopter.'

Lillian was studying her reflection in the mirror beside the front door. She checked her lipstick and put a comb to her hair to tease it a few more times before leaving. I watched her precise immersion in her own good looks, her apparently careless manipulation of them. We were lucky, I thought; after all these years we were still attracted to each other. We still found stimulation and comfort in each other's company.

'Photographs will spur your imagination,' she said.

'Hopefully,' I answered, although in truth I had been unable to settle on even a provisional idea for the land. In desperation I had sketched geometries pirated from Japanese gardens, barbican siege patterns and printed circuits, but even these simple parodies had been lifeless.

I picked up the handwritten envelope again. It was so well sealed that I had to tear it across the front to extract the contents. Inside were three small neatly-folded pages, covered with attractive, precise handwriting in blue ink. A woman's name and address were written in capitals in the upper corner, as if I would wish to record them. I did not recognise either.

I read the first few lines. The floor trembled.

I folded the pages back together as quickly as I could. They did not sit evenly, and could not be fitted back in the torn envelope. I reopened the pages, fumbled with the edges, refolded them. I tried again to replace them. The angle of the tear was difficult and it took me several attempts before I succeeded. All the time I kept my head down, scared that if I looked up Lillian would see the shock in my face.

'Who's it from?' she asked.

'No one special,' I said, my voice as ghostly as a message on burned paper.

Dear Mr McGoldrick, the letter began, *I am sorry to write to you so unexpectedly, but if you are the Michael James McGoldrick I think you are, then I have reason to believe that you are my father.*

Now I tried to thrust the envelope into my shirt pocket, but it seemed too large and inflexible to fit. Each time I tried the paper crumpled with a noise that sounded like a poster being ripped from a wall. I was suffocatingly aware of Lillian's presence, her interest. When I had read Eve's last note there had been no one to watch me.

Quite suddenly there was a feeling of lightness in my head. Either the room swayed or I did, I was not sure, and the blood contracted towards my heart. I made one last successful attempt to thrust the letter into my pocket. Lillian walked across the room and gripped my arm. I knew she had moved swiftly, but time was distorting and the sound of her footfalls trailed behind her like lazy followers.

'Are you all right?' she asked anxiously.

I tried to nod, but did not know if I had even moved. I had the sensation of floating in salt-rich water; my limbs were buoyant but inflexible.

Lillian steered me to a chair, gently pressed on my shoulder to make me sit down, and pushed my head down between my knees. The room collapsed in on itself.

I came to, not knowing if I had blacked out for a second

or for half an hour. Into my mind came the thought that dying might be like this.

'Jamie? You fainted for about ten seconds.'

I said nothing; the musculature of my jaw was heavy.

'Should I call a doctor?'

I shook my head.

'What's wrong? Can you tell me?'

I managed to speak, but the words were breathless. 'I'll be all right. Give me a few minutes.'

'I've never seen you like this. Are you sure you're all right?'

'I'll be fine.'

'You don't look it.'

'Maybe been worrying too much. About the commission.'

'But you've never done that in all the time we've been together. You're not a worrier.'

'Don't know why. Just one of those things. I'm getting better now. I can feel it.'

It was true. My mind and body had been eerily unreal for several seconds, but now the attack was passing almost as quickly as it had arrived.

'Just one of those things,' I repeated. I thought that perhaps all the colour had drained from my cheeks, so I put my hands on my face to shield it.

Lillian made me more tea while I sat as quietly as a patient. She watched me all the time. I knew what she was thinking; she was worried that this could be the herald of a later, more serious attack. It was true that I was also frightened, but it was the opening sentence of the letter that was crowding everything else from my mind.

'Who was it from?' she asked after a while.

I feigned inocence. 'What?'

'The letter. The letter you were reading when you had that turn.'

I looked round as if searching for it.

'You put it in your shirt pocket,' she said.

I let my fingers stray there idly. I wanted Lillian to believe that the letter was so unimportant that I had half-forgotten it. The edge of the envelope was as menacing as a drawn blade.

I took away my hand and nodded absent-mindedly. In my professional life I was used to distortion and petty falsehood, but with Lillian I had been honest for a long time. There was only one part of my life that I had disguised. Now I was being forced into more lies.

'It's just an old student wanting a reference,' I said. 'I'll have to think about what I can say about him.'

'Him? It looked like a woman's handwriting.'

'Did I say *him*? Stupid of me. It's a woman.'

'You speak as if you're not sure how to answer.'

'No,' I agreed, 'I'm not. Shouldn't you be leaving?'

'Only if you're well.'

'I'm well. I swear it.'

'Jamie, I don't want to leave you on your own. There's no one here today. Even the cleaning lady has her day off.'

My concentration had been drawn back to the letter, and I hardly heard Lillian speak.

'I'll ring Ken Takama, and Terry Evans as well,' she said firmly. 'I'll tell them you can't make it.'

'No, don't do that. I promise I'll do it myself if I'm still even slightly unwell. But I'm not. I'm almost fully recovered.'

'Really?' she asked sceptically.

'Yes. Really.'

'You're going to go, aren't you?'

I reached out, took her hand and squeezed it. 'I have to. I've got to get started on this project. I've delayed too long already. You've told me as much yourself.'

Lillian left for work shortly afterwards. When she had gone I went to the upper floor of the house where I had my studio workroom. I locked the door behind me and tested the handle like a thief who fears interruption and discovery. There were plans, preliminary sketches, and a few rejected maquettes strewn across the desk. I moved them to one side to expose a patch of bare surface. Then I took the letter from my pocket, held it by the corner as if it were contaminated, and dropped it onto the space that I had cleared.

I walked to the window and stared out over the bare trees. The city tower-blocks, spires, masts were greyish blue in the late winter light. I thought of people, and space, and years – seven million people, seven hundred square miles, and a quarter of a century. It had been understandable, no, rational for me to be certain that my daughter would never track me down. I had taken every necessary step. I had insisted that her new parents would not be told her original surname. And yet here in this room was a message from someone I believed I had cast out of my life for ever.

Minutes passed before I returned to the desk and sat down. I studied the tear in the envelope. It was in the shape of a fatal wound, a shark attack perhaps, which had left the victim's innards exposed to light.

A tortured man will dream that his anguish is not real but a nightmare he is on the brink of waking from. In the same way I dared to hope that, unaccountably and miraculously, time would somehow loop, that it would be an hour ago, and that when the mail arrived the letter would not be among it.

Then I tried to convince myself that I had misread the first sentence. Perhaps it had been innocuous, mundane, not from my daughter at all; perhaps when I read the words again I would be able to laugh at my own foolishness.

But I did not open the envelope because I knew that my hopes were groundless and that the words were exactly as I remembered them. I was hanging onto the present while my whole life plunged into the dark, engulfing sea of my past.

I put my fingertips to the tear and gently widened it so that I could see the outer page. The ink on its obverse showed through the blank side like a faded manuscript. My imagination, still seeking runnels of escape, conjured a sudden magical illegibility. But I knew that I would have to read the remainder of the letter or my dreams would never let me rest.

It must have taken another minute to summon courage. Eventually I seized the envelope and roughly extracted the three pages as if they meant nothing to me at all.

She had everything correct; her mother's name, mine, the occupations we had given (*artist* and *student*; we had laughed about it), her original name, Grace. Her exact date of birth I had forgotten, but the month and the year were accurate. Whatever had happened to my daughter, she had somehow been given a copy of her original birth certificate.

I recognise that it is possible that you and I have nothing to do with each other, and that a coincidence of name and location has led me to make a terrible and unforgivable error. I recognise, too, that if you are *my biological father then you may want to have nothing to do with me. You must have had good reasons for doing what you did, and you may not wish to meet me now. You may think that I am being crazily presumptuous in approaching you. So if you do not answer this letter I will do my best to understand. I'll think of you as having torn it up, and I'll never try to contact you again.*

But if I am right, and if you want to meet me, you have my name, my address, my telephone number. Contact me in whatever way you think best. If you telephone and someone else answers, they will be able to find me.

Or it may be that you do not want to meet, but only to know about my life; this, too, I would try to understand.

I think that I should write no more just now. This must have given you a shock. I'm sorry about that. I considered various ways of approaching you, but in the end this seemed the least painful. If you are the man who twenty-five years ago had a child called Grace, and if you have spent years wondering what happened to her, then I can tell you that she has spent much of her adolescence and her adult life wondering about her real father and mother.

I have made the first move; I leave the next one to you. I'm waiting.

The letter was signed with her new name – *Judith Ford.*

I refolded it, laid it on the desk as carefully as a fragile relic, and put my hands to my head. After a few seconds I discovered that I had placed my fingers over the pulse in my temple. I could sense the rhythm of my own body, and I could not help but think of the same rhythm beating in hers.

Suddenly independent and imperious, I tore the letter into four pieces and dropped them into the wastepaper basket. I could have torn it smaller, beyond recovery, but perhaps I already knew that in five or ten minutes' time I would be on my knees, lifting the quarters from where I had tossed them, ready to seal them together with transparent tape.

And I was reminded of a craftsman assembling a stained-glass window, fixing his pieces in their pre-ordained pattern, making a barrier through which light would continue to fall, but could never fall in the same way as before.

Later that morning I set off for the Peermain estate. It was an hour's drive from the city, and for all that time my mind was on the letter. I could discover no path, reach no conclusion. Decision and mastery were beyond me. I was bound to the treadmill of my own imagination.

Terry Evans's church had once been part of the estate, but now it was isolated in its own small grounds by the roadside. A strong breeze bent the tops of the conifers that grew on the far side of the boundary wall at the back of the church. They screened off a view across parkland that had once been painted by Gainsborough. I pulled onto the gravel in front of the door only to find two sleek black cars parked there. Steel bars gleamed in the rear of the first; it was a hearse. From the church came the sound of organ music but no singing.

An expressionless man in a grey suit and black tie sat behind the wheel of the taxi. In an oddly hopeful voice he asked if I was a relative. I told him I was not, and asked if the church was full. He shook his head and smirked knowingly. I took this to mean that it was almost empty.

I sidled through the open door. The church was deserted except for an organist and the small group of people clustered around a coffin in front of the altar. Terry Evans projected his voice as if all the pews were full, but it echoed hollowly around an empty nave. There was no one present except clergy and undertakers.

I sat down in the pew nearest the door, but as soon as I did the service ended and I had to stand up again. Organ music rolled and echoed around the deserted church as the coffin was trundled back down the aisle. One of the trolley wheels squeaked on each rotation. There were only two wreaths on the lid, and I guessed that these had been donated by the church and by the undertakers. I was the only person there who was not an official.

Terry approached the door with his black-bound prayer book clutched in his hands and his round, pleasant face set in dutiful solemnity. He maintained this demeanour until the coffin was over the threshold, and then he turned to raise his eyebrows at me.

Unsure of procedure, I smiled and nodded.

'You're late,' he murmured; 'I have to see to this.'

The coffin was lifted from its collapsible trolley and loaded into the back of the hearse. Wind crackled the cellophane on the flowers and lifted Terry's swatch of carefully-brushed sandy hair from his bald spot.

'Should we meet at the vicarage?' he asked. 'I know the cemetery is out of your way. The undertakers will bring me back. I'll only be about twenty minutes.'

'Is anyone going with the body?' I asked.

'Only ourselves.'

'No one else?'

'Sadly.'

I made up my mind. 'I'll come along.'

He nodded approvingly. 'That would be a Christian response.'

I got back into my car and followed the tiny cortège to the cemetery a mile away. I knew nothing at all about the person who was being interred, so I remembered events from my own past. The sculptures that had first brought me recognition were a series of concrete slots set into the earth, like petrified gravespaces.

At the cemetery the wind was stronger. It shivered the moss-dark yews and flapped the black coats of the undertaker's men so that they looked like injured birds. We followed an asphalt pathway between polished marble headstones laid out like tiny megaliths. At the end of the walk I found myself unnervingly close to the open grave. The soil was piled up on one side, protected by a tarpaulin. Nearby were the squares of turf that would be relaid and trodden down when the hole was filled.

Eve had been cremated; the last burial I had attended was my parents'. On that day, too, the wind had been high. My father, who had been killed as soon as the steering column punctured his chest, was placed in his coffin at the bottom of the grave; my mother, who had survived the crash for about twelve hours, was laid on top of him. The brass nameplate had gleamed from the trench like a last signal; I could read her name quite clearly.

And I could read this man's, too. Archie Sproat. It seemed an appropriate name for such a sad and faintly ridiculous burial. The flaked gold lettering on the grey marble headstone showed that his wife and daughter had died a long time before he did.

Because I felt it was expected of me I took a handful of soil and threw it on the coffin. The wind had dried the soil so that much of it blew away as dust, but some heavier clumps hit the lid with a curiously menacing noise. I tried to imagine the face of the man lying there, encased in darkness, the soil piled up in a mound to one side of his last resting place, but I had nothing at all to go on apart from his name, and that made me think of someone ordinary, possibly even ugly, with little achievement behind him. It was an unfair and demeaning way to picture anyone.

I looked again at the dates on the headstone, and only now did I comprehend them fully. Archie Sproat's wife had been dead for forty years, and his daughter had been dead for forty-one. Although the daughter's date of birth was given, there was no full date for her death. Instead only the month and year were quoted; it was the year after she was born. I felt suddenly cold and turned away to walk down the path.

Terry was waiting for me a few yards away, his swatch of hair standing at an alertly boyish angle. 'That was kind of you,' he said, shaking my hand. 'I've never had a funeral before where no one turned up.'

'Solitary, was he?'

'You hadn't heard of him?'

'I don't spend too much time here. And what I do spend isn't occupied by local gossip. I'm sorry I'm late, Terry; I was unexpectedly delayed. I rang but your wife said you'd already left. Look, I'll drive you back to the vicarage if you like. It's easier.'

He accepted my offer, shook hands with the undertaker and his men, and then we drove away.

We had little in common, but I liked Terry Evans. He made it plain that he found my work difficult to appreciate, but nevertheless he would always help me if he could. In return, I had to pretend to agree that most individuals were, in essence, good-hearted. Sometimes, too, I had to pretend to understand him when he talked about theologians and philosophers. Like many of the people who were now my friends, he assumed that my intelligence was sharper than it actually was. When I had been putting together a book about my work, Terry had even provided me with quotes on the nature of perception and the role of the observer. They had all seemed too forbidding, and eventually I had chosen as an epigraph something from Berkeley which seemed both germane and ambiguous – *Truth is the cry of all, but the game of the few.* I wasn't sure that I fully understood this. If ever I was questioned about it all I did was smile as knowingly as the chauffeur outside the church.

'I wanted to tell you about the wood on the estate,' I explained. 'We're going to clear out the centre. I thought you might like to know.'

'What do you mean, clear out?'

'Maybe the phrase is too dramatic. I mean that some of the trees will be cut down. But more than two-thirds, and possibly more than three-quarters, will be left standing. There are no reasons not to do it. The Ordnance Survey maps show a small copse, nothing more. The older maps show nothing. The wood must have grown wild in the days of the last of the Peermains.'

Terry was unconvinced. 'There are few good reasons for cutting down trees these days.'

'And making room for a work of art is one of them.'

'I don't think I could entirely concur. What will you do with the timber?'

I had not even thought of that. 'Cabinet-makers will want it,' I improvised.

'Really?'

'Look,' I said, 'the idea is that people will be able to pick their way through the wood to reach a sculpture at the very centre. Of course the path will have to be upgraded and maintained. We'll edge it with stone or wood and cut channels for rainwater drainage. I want people to be able to go there whatever the weather. For one thing, to truly appreciate sculpture in the environment you have to see it under snow.'

'You say people. But, you know, you're working on a private estate. It's out of bounds to most of us. As for a path, I expect you'll have trouble even finding one through the wood. An animal trail, perhaps.'

For as long as I had been friendly with Terry he had expressed doubts about my sponsors. Ironically, Lillian and I had first met him at a party to celebrate the restoration of the old house. The food had been internationalised British with tricksy Japanese-American additions; when Ken Takama entertained me, it was usually internationalised Japanese with European wines. Terry had been at the party with several dozen other local worthies. I had been present as an artist who had worked for the company, at sites across the world, on and off for more than twenty years.

Then, and subsequently, Terry complained that few local people were employed at the old hall, that the conifers were an unnecessary and ugly blocking of a classic view across parkland, and that video cameras and security patrols made anyone visiting the house uneasy. It seemed to me, on the other hand, that ownership by a Japanese electronics company was an improvement on ownership by a faded aristocracy. The last Peermain had declined to a premature old age with the building rotting around him and his land running to seed. Vagrants slept in the ruined outhouses and poachers roamed the park. Now the estate was being gradually restored and improved, and although boundaries had been erected round it, anyone could visit providing they asked in advance.

We drove through a small village. The new owners of the estate had donated money for the rebuilding of the village hall, and to the various shows and fêtes that had once again become part of their life. Ten miles away, on the outskirts of a new town, the company's electronics factory provided hundreds of people with employment.

'Don't you feel that to put up a sculpture in the middle of a restricted wood is rather, well, rarefied?' Terry asked after a while.

'Art history is full of examples of work that was only seen by an élite. That's the way that progress was made. And anyone can see my work if they really want to.'

He gave a small hum of qualified assent. It was a uniquely clerical sound, and it made me try to further justify myself.

'Look,' I went on, 'obviously I want my work to be seen by as many people as possible. But you can understand my sponsors' caution. And I need them and people like them to commission me – it's the way I make a lot of my money. But I'm not just telling you out of friendship or duty. There's the mound.'

'The mound in the wood?'

'The fact is,' I said, 'I'll have to landscape it in some way. I can't let something as big as a house remain untouched. It will mess up the sightlines. And I certainly don't want to put a statue on top; that would look too much like a monument.'

He said nothing.

'I may even have to flatten it,' I confessed.

'Are you asking if I approve? It's company land, not the church's.'

'It must be a spoil heap. If the wood was originally a coppice, that would make sense. But there's a small depression on the top. That doesn't seem to fit in with anything natural.'

'Do you think it had something to do with lime-kilns, bloomeries, that kind of thing?'

'I was hoping you could tell me definitely. You know the area better than most.'

'Doesn't Ken Takama know? He's having the history of the estate written. By a university lecturer, I'm told. She must be a research specialist.'

'I think I'd rather rely on whatever you could tell me, Terry.'

'You compliment me. But I'm sure Mr Takama could provide you with better sources. He'll be fascinated by such details. You know what Americans are like for heritage.'

'Ken's not typical. He's got an American passport, but his parents were Japanese and he took his degree in England. I was told he'd changed his name so that Westerners could pronounce it more easily. He hasn't even got an American accent.'

'You mean he's international? Just like you've become?'

I did not know if this was a compliment or a jibe, so I ignored it.

'He still doesn't know about the mound.'

'Truthfully, Jamie, I don't know what it is either. But I'm not aware of anything significant about it.'

We discussed possibilities as I drove. Most of them were far too adventurous for a mound so humble that maps made no mention of it. Nor, as far as Terry was aware, had any cultural or historical interest ever been expressed. This seemed to exclude fortifications and barrows. We agreed, finally, that the mound was probably either a geological quirk of some kind, like a moraine or a tiny drumlin, or that it was the consequence of vanished industrial activity, perhaps mining or charcoal burning, that had been encouraged on the Peermains' land and then expelled from it.

'You're asking me to have a word with a few people,' Terry said as we approached the vicarage.

'Yes. Diplomatically. Just to see if there *is* anything I should be told.'

'You know, I think you may be frightened of having a preservation order slapped on you for either the wood or the mound. Is that true?'

I stopped the car at the edge of the gravel path leading up to the vicarage, but left the engine running.

'You've got me,' I said. 'That's right.'

He hummed again. 'I know a few local historians and archaeologists. I suppose I could have a quiet word with them and come back to you. It may take weeks. Is that all right?'

I nodded. 'The trees will be cleared as soon as I decide on a final shape for the piece. I'm having aerial photographs taken soon. That will give me a better idea of the contours.'

'It seems that you'll be rushing ahead anyway.'

'Sculpture can never be rushed.'

It was a pat response, and I could tell Terry recognised it as such.

'I'll come back to you,' he repeated. 'And thank you for attending the burial. The last part of Mr Sproat's life was very sad. He lay dead for a while before he was discovered.'

'He had no friends?'

His left hand was on the door handle. 'Not in the last forty years or so.'

'Good God,' I said. I thought of all the villagers getting on with their lives, and not one of them bothering to turn up for a neighbour's burial. 'Is there no more family?' I asked.

'He was the last,' Terry said, lifting the handle and easing the door open. 'His wife died of a broken heart, they say. She never recovered from the death of their daughter. She always thought it was his fault.'

I was suddenly, irrationally queasy.

'You and I are fortunate never to have suffered such a loss,' he said as he stood on the path with one hand still holding the door open.

'Yes,' I said, 'we're lucky.' I wanted to drive away quickly in case he looked at my face and saw betrayal in it. But Terry wanted a few last words.

'It must do terrible things to a person,' he mused as he closed the door.

'It must,' I agreed. The door clicked shut.

Terry raised his hand in farewell and walked towards the vicarage. I drove away immediately, my head full of memories, without checking in my rear-view mirror.

There was a scream of tyres, I automatically pressed hard on the brake, my seat-belt locked. A car, travelling along the road I had just driven, shuddered to a halt a few inches away from me. For a suspended moment its driver and I looked in shock at each other through the windows. Then, collecting himself, he shook his head in contempt at my stupidity and drove away.

I waited until he was out of sight round the bend before I pulled further onto the road and then drove away slowly.

Black ornamental gates stood open at the entrance to the estate. I slowed at the gatehouse to let the security guard check my registration and then I followed the long curve of the drive to the house.

One component of my Interlocking Pieces was set on the lawn like a toppled colossus. A peacock strutted along the crest, the ragged besom of its tail folded and lowered, while around the base a few peahens pecked at imaginary food. Behind the wooden sculpture the parkland swept away in a gradual decline, until it rose again towards the screen of conifers and the half-hidden spire of Terry Evans's church. Another Interlocking Piece was positioned just to the left of the geometric centre of the vista, and still further left the ground rose again until its swell was hidden by a copse of bare trees. Within their wintry protection lay the mound.

I parked beside the house and then walked up its broad front steps. A television camera drew a bead on me from its fixture above the door. Once inside the house I signed the log at reception and sat waiting for Ken Takama. I had to leaf through one of the company's glossily expensive brochures for about ten minutes before he appeared.

'Jamie,' he said in his unplaceable accent as he shook my hand too vigorously. 'Look, I'm sorry, but you're late and I have a meeting that I can't leave.'

'I'm sorry, Ken; I wasn't able to set off until a lot later than planned. I was taken ill.'

His broad, flat face showed no concern, but a slight increase in the tension of his shoulders indicated a sudden wariness.

'It was nothing serious,' I added quickly. 'I'm over it now.'

Ken was a thickset, bulky man with a short neck. He had trained with weights in his youth; when he nodded, as he did now, it always seemed that his chin would touch his chest in an unconscious parody of an ancestral salute.

'You'll not be able to join me in taking another look at the site?' I asked, knowing his answer must be No.

'I can't just now. But I have that aerial shoot arranged for next week; I'll send you the prints. So what I need from you is the concept, a schedule, and notes towards a costing. You can do that for me soon, can't you?'

'As soon as I can, Ken,' I answered, as if there were no problems at all with the site.

I said my goodbyes, went back outside and walked across the parkland towards the next Interlocking Piece. Shadows of clouds slid over the grass like rays across an ocean floor.

A spatter of bright crocuses had appeared between the sculpture and the wood. I walked around them and then bore left towards the trees and the hidden mound. The ground rose slightly; the mound sat on the apex of its swell like a boss in the centre of a shield.

There was still a discernible path between the trees, although it was partly screened by rhododendron bushes which had spread unchecked throughout the wood. Above them a few withered leaves still hung on stripped branches. They might have been the ragged standards of a vanquished year. I followed the pathway's gentle rise through birches scabbed with seaweed-coloured lichen. The new buds were dull, tight, and unbroken. High branches, harried by the wind, struck against each other like men fighting with staves.

Soon the grassy outcrop of the mound rose from among the trees. Its mossy flanks were now being colonised by saplings. I chose one of the strongest, used it to pull myself up the side, and then scrambled onto the top.

The summit was circular, with a slight depression at its centre. Within the bowl a few snowdrops were growing; their whiteness was startlingly pure against the verdigris moss. The mound was definitely artificial, I thought gloomily; nature in England did not specialise in this kind of symmetry.

And then my pessimism fell away. Of what concern was it to me if the mound was judged to be of historic importance? It was on private land; it did not appear on maps; I could do what I wanted with it. What did it matter if my abandoned daughter had finally tracked me down? I had risen far above my past. I was rich; I had influence. I had rid myself of her once; a second time would be even easier.

The wind cuffed my shoulders and riffled the hair on my head as I looked across the wood. From this height I could just see the upper part of the house roof. All around me the naked branches swayed like submarine growths in a tidal swell.

2

For the next week I lived with uncertainty. I forced myself to take decisions that I knew should be irrevocable, but which remained firm for only a few minutes. I would write to tell Judith Ford that she was mistaken and that she should never contact me again. I would telephone her to admit that she was right, but that I had no wish to meet or to know anything about her. I would destroy her letter, this time completely, erasing it forever from my memory just as I had tried to erase her.

During this period I said nothing to Lillian. How could I? I had lied about my past since the day I met her.

On several occasions I rang Judith's number, or began to. I picked up the telephone and quickly replaced it. I dialled and cut the line before the connection was made. Once I even hung up when I heard the first burr of the ringing tone. Each time I rang I keyed in the code that guaranteed my call could not be traced back to me.

Eventually, at last, not knowing if I were a wise man or a fool, I rang and held on until she answered.

She gave her name.

As soon as I heard it I knew that she had been hoping I would ring; otherwise she would never have identified herself to an unknown caller. I was struck, too, by her accent. It was different to both mine and her mother's.

And yet it was absurd that I should expect any similarity. Our daughter had grown up in different places and among different people. I had no reason to hear an echo.

'My name's Jamie McGoldrick,' I said. I had intended the announcement to be flat, but instead it was sheared as clearly as a geological fault.

For a few seconds neither of us spoke. I was slightly dizzy and thought again of a damaged vessel. Beneath my feet the floor canted, and the walls around me shifted from the vertical.

Nothing was said. To regain my balance I stared at a photograph on my wall. It showed bright sand being poured into a square hole in an Alpine glacier. I had cut the hole carefully, so that it would hold a cubic metre, no more.

Still nothing was said. I thought that we could become locked in a silence neither of us could break. We stood in our rooms as if in cells, each imagining how the other looked and what they were doing, with no clues other than faint breaths rustling in the earpiece like dry leaves blown across a floor.

And then we both spoke at the same time. I told Judith that I had received her letter and she said she was glad I had called.

We stopped, perhaps to let the other continue, perhaps because each comment had been unnecessary. I saw us either falling into a silence even more profound and unbreakable or continuing to talk across each other like crazed actors rehearsing a parable of isolation.

'I didn't know if you would ring,' she said.

'I thought about ignoring your letter. I still don't know if I'm doing the right thing.'

And suddenly I was furious at Judith Ford. What right had she to approach me in such a way? Had she not considered the disruption she could cause? We had nothing in common but the blind, thoughtless logic of genetics; whatever else we may have shared had been destroyed a quarter of a century ago. Like invaders who efface a statue, so her new parents had even destroyed the name we had chosen for her. And yet this intruder, this stranger, had ransacked my peace and set the past to maraud through my dreams.

'Let's be honest with each other,' I went on. 'I can tell you right now that I don't want to meet you. I have nothing to do with you and you have nothing to do with me. We shared a few months together, months you're incapable of remembering and I've done my best to forget. To me you're less important that a forgotten holiday. To you I must be the father who cared so little that he got rid of you. Those may not be pleasant facts, but at least they're ones we can live by.'

The pattern of her breathing changed; I had wounded her.

The anger I had thought was limitless was suddenly discharged, vanishing as quickly as it had arrived. I had succumbed to rage and now I felt mean-spirited. There had been a better way to do this. I should have been sympathetic, measured, apparently conciliatory, but nevertheless firm in my rejection of Judith.

'I'm sorry, but you must see the sense of my argument,' I continued. I was incapable of being anything other than brusque.

Still she did not answer.

'Don't you agree with me?'

'How can I? If I'd thought that I would never have written.'

This time it was I who said nothing.

'I don't think you realise how much courage I needed to write that letter. You obviously can't imagine how long it took me to decide that I should do it. You don't know about the days I spent wondering what to say and how to say it. I must have started and stopped more than a hundred times. You don't have any grasp of that, do you, Mr McGoldrick?'

I would have expected her to call me nothing else, but I was still disturbed by her formal use of my last name.

I told myself I was being irrational. An impassioned *Father* or, even worse, a sentiment-rich *Dad* would have been much more difficult to cope with.

She went on.

'I took a lot of trouble. I didn't want you to think I was either an icy genealogist or a driven neurotic. Why? Because I wanted to make you *want* to contact me. I realised that you might not want to meet, not just yet. Even though I would have been disappointed I would still have understood. In the end I thought the balance of the words was right, as right as I could get it. I sealed the envelope and taped it. And I posted it before I was tempted to make yet another alteration. I posted it and I waited for you to respond.'

'I see,' I said colourlessly.

'But I must have made a terrible miscalculation. My letter can't have been that provocative. My assumption must have been wrong to begin with. And my hope must have been groundless. I didn't think you would treat me so brutally. Even silence would be better than insult. I know my mother's dead – that's right, isn't it?'

There had been a note of uncertainty in her voice, as if she did not know how to test me further.

'You were only a few months old when she died.'

My confirmation did not distress her; there was only a moment's pause before she continued.

'For years I've wondered what my real father was like. I think I have the answer now. I no longer need to meet you.'

'No,' I said, 'wait.'

I could not picture Judith standing there so I pictured her mother instead.

'Please,' I said, believing this would stop her putting down the telephone.

She did not say anything.

'This has been a terrible shock for me,' I confessed. 'It took you a long time to write, and it's taken me a while to decide to respond. Perhaps our reasons aren't all that different.'

I did not know why I was so eager to appease. A prudent man, aware of the values and patterns of his own life, would never have encouraged an invasion such as hers. Something else had begun to shape my responses, something uncontrollable and barely conscious.

'I don't know if I should sympathise,' she said with a sulkiness belonging to someone much younger than her years. 'Perhaps you make a habit of rejection. You could be that kind of person.'

'I'm not. Really I'm not.'

'But I don't know that, do I? We don't know anything about each other. Maybe you were right. Maybe it would have been better for both of us if I had never found out about you.'

She lapsed into silence.

'What do you want me to do now?' I asked.

'You know the answer to that.'

'You want to meet me.'

She was getting what she wanted. I felt I could detect a pleasure in her silence.

'Why?' I protested. 'What purpose would it serve? Hasn't this conversation told us enough?'

'If it does nothing else, it will lay a ghost. I'd like you to tell me about my mother. And something about yourself. And I'd like to look into your face and see if I recognise myself in it.'

'You're mine, all right. There's no doubt about that. Whatever your mother's problems, infidelity wasn't one of them.'

'I'd still like to look at you.'

'And me? What would I get?'

'The newspaper profile mentioned your adopted daughter. Are there no others?'

'None. Claire's an only child.'

'Apart from me – and I'm your *real* child. The only one who has inherited your blood, your genes, maybe even the way you look. You can see for yourself how you've passed on parts of your identity to the next generation. You're bound to be curious about that. Everyone is.'

'Listen, I've got no interest in answering painful questions. You've already opened an old wound. I don't want it deepened.'

'Are you agreeing we should meet?'

'No, I'm not. Let me think about it.'

'And ring me back, you mean? Don't call us, we'll call you? That sounds like another way of refusing me.'

'I'm not refusing you. I said I'd think—'

'You've already had a week to think. You know we should meet. You may not want to, but it's your duty. Things have gone too far for us *not* to meet.'

'All right then, I'll meet you.' Exasperation rang through my voice like a struck bell. She spoke before its echo died away.

'We'll decide a time and a place. We'll decide it now. And we'll both be there. We'll not let the other down. Is it a deal?'

I hesitated for a second.

'Is it a deal?' she asked again.

'Yes,' I said, 'it's a deal.'

It was not easy to agree a suitable meeting place. It seemed absurd that a father and daughter, even if separated by time and history, should have to decide on somewhere that was public but not too crowded. In the end we agreed, prosaically, to meet at the official rendezvous point of a railway station.

I arrived fifteen minutes early and prowled a high, wide concourse that echoed like a marshalling yard. I wondered if Judith was doing the same. Perhaps when we finally met we would realise that only a few minutes before we had unknowingly passed by each other. Every time I pretended to look at a magazine or study the electronic announcement boards I kept an eye on our meeting place. One or two individuals paused there, looked around and moved away, but none seemed as if they might be my daughter. Then a band of elderly holidaymakers congregated under the sign for several minutes, half-lost until a tour representative with a clipboard drew them close together and shepherded them away. At that moment the rendezvous area was deserted. I looked at my watch; it was time.

I sauntered across, paused beneath the sign and then, defensively, took up a position slightly to one side of it.

In front of me hundreds of travellers crisscrossed the concourse, their shadows darkening its pale surface like migrating birds. I wondered how long I would allow myself to stand there before walking away. I checked my watch even though there was a gigantic digital clock above the departure and arrival displays. I had been there less than two minutes and yet I was already beginning to construct excuses to leave.

When I looked up a woman in a dark coat, split black skirt and boots was walking steadily towards me.

We recognised each other immediately. Our eyes locked like enemies, like lovers. We hid within our own unflickering stares, each parrying the other's examination as the distance between us narrowed and the noise of her heels striking the imitation marble grew louder.

It took me only a few seconds to decide that she was more like her mother than me – the same straight dark hair, pale skin, high cheekbones, narrow face. Judith even walked with the brisk confidence that had punctuated Eve's periods of despair; her body, too, must be similar.

'I needn't ask,' she said, 'I know who you are.' There was no trace of query in her voice and her eyes held a challenge. They were dark, too; just like Eve's.

I held out my hand even though I had previously decided not to. She hesitated and then touched it briefly, as if she feared that an overwhelming current would flow out of me if she kept the contact longer.

I remembered the last time we had touched. She had been only a few months old, and hardly distinguishable from other children of her age. To see her again, to touch her after all those years, was to have a sudden vertiginous insight into the processes of survival, growth, even death.

'I wasn't sure you would keep your promise,' she said.

'If I hadn't, would you have tried to contact me again?'

'It would have been wiser not to.'

'But would you?'

'Probably.'

I shifted position, as uncomfortable as a man whose every movement is being studied. 'Where shall we go now?' I asked, wanting it over with quickly.

'I thought you would be the one with ideas.'

'I don't know. A café? The park?'

'They're possibles.'

'Well?'

'I know; why don't you take me to the zoo?'

I did not know if she was being serious.

'That's where fathers take the children they've abandoned, isn't it?' she asked.

I thought of objecting that she was far too mature to think of herself in such terms. Instead I said that the zoo was a taxi ride away and no longer cheap to enter.

'You're not quibbling, are you? Surely you don't begrudge me a few hours or few pounds?'

I was unsure where her responses lay on the scale between jocularity and high seriousness, but I reluctantly agreed to her suggestion.

We walked to the rank without further conversation. In the back of the taxi we looked out of opposite windows, but sometimes we stole a glance at each other and then turned away sharply, like criminals unable to face their victims.

After a while Judith slipped on a pair of dark glasses with large circular lenses. Then she broke the silence.

'And how is Lillian?'

'What do you know about her?'

'Only what I read.'

'She's fine,' I said cautiously.

'She's a lecturer, isn't she?'

'Something like that.'

In the rearview mirror I saw the driver's eyes flick across us before they returned to the road ahead.

When I was a child I had been taken with my school class to the nearest city zoo, two hours travelling away from where I lived. I could still recall how my senses became keyed up by excitement. I was unsure if the arrangement of terraces, houses and cages was a place or an event. I even imagined that, like an enchanted city, it might somehow stand outside of time. I studied the zoo like a cartographer; it made me imagine extravagant terrains whose glamour was always marked by squalor, dung, scattered food. In the monkey house I found myself being watched by animals whose facial musculature and patterns of behaviour seemed, in a way in which I could not quite understand, to echo characteristics which I knew I shared.

'Is there any special part you want to go to?' I asked Judith as we left the ticket office.

'You still come here. What do you recommend?'

At first I did not realise how she knew this, and I wondered if some aspect of my behaviour had betrayed me. Then I remembered that in the newspaper profile I had mentioned that I sometimes visited the zoo.

'I don't recommend anything,' I told her. 'Should we just follow the main pathways?'

'Yes, we'll do that. And stop where we want. But let's start with the bird enclosure.'

The high aviary was constructed of metal struts and mesh, and peaked and crested like a Bedouin tent. To me it resembled the haul a marauding sea-god might make if he cast his net across the masts of docked galleys. We pushed through thin rustling curtains of chain and found ourselves on an elevated walkway leading through the enclosure. Trapped birds swooped through the geometrical spaces and perched and nested on the soiled aluminium spars.

Just before an angle in the walkway Judith stopped, leaned on the galvanised metal rail, and looked down. There was a fall of thirty feet or more to the floor of the aviary, and for a moment she looked like a hesitant suicide at the parapet of a bridge.

'How did you know who I was?' I asked.

'It was easy.'

'Easy?'

'You're a public figure.'

'Hardly that.'

'Public enough to have profiles written about you.'

'That can't have given me away. I said nothing about you or your mother.'

'No. But there was a half-page portrait that looked a bit like me. It said your name was Michael James McGoldrick.

I knew my father's full name. It had to be more than coincidence.'

'You were told who your real parents were?'

I could not see Judith's eyes behind her dark glasses. The only emotion came through her voice, her stance, the occasional tightening of her lips.

'I didn't know I was adopted, although I was suspicious. The Fords were very religious and very self-righteous. They lied to me until I was sixteen. We were having a furious argument. They told me my bad side was getting the upper hand. I had the usual adolescent logic; I said I must have inherited my behaviour from them. And suddenly they told me I was adopted. I'd been suspicious for so long that when I was finally told the truth I didn't believe it. But they had a copy of my birth certificate. The real one.'

'They weren't supposed to have that.'

'They had it all right. They threw it at me as if they were ashamed of it. And as if I should be, too.'

'You've done nothing about me for years. Why now?'

'I'd thought about you. Sometimes days passed without me thinking of anything else. One day I even went to the address on the certificate, but it's a street of newly-built shops. The owners don't know what happened five years ago, let alone twenty-five. I suppose I could have registered to trace you, but for quite a while I had no fixed address, so tracing was always something I was going to do in the future. For years all I could do was brood.'

She was quiet for a while, and then went on.

'The trouble with an unknown past is that it has no shape, no form. That doesn't stop it from swallowing up your present. When I opened that newspaper and saw your face I knew that the past was showing itself to me. It was a kind of revelation. I could feel it growing at the edge of my consciousness. And with each line I read, the clearer it became.'

'And that's how you know about Lillian. And the zoo.'

'It said you came here to study animal architecture – burrows, nests, that sort of thing. Is that right?'

'I've been here a few times. Sometimes you can get ideas from watching how animals help create their environment – nests and tunnels, for instance. And contemporary zoo architecture is so specialised that sometimes I get ideas from that.'

'Like here?'

Yes, I thought, like here, and I looked up towards an apex of the aviary. Storks had nested on a junction of grey struts, and high in the pyramidal reaches small birds fluttered ineffectively towards the sun.

'I've memorised just about every word of that profile,' Judith said.

'I wouldn't put too much trust in it. It's always a temptation to tell a reporter only what you think they want to know.'

'I don't put much trust in it. How could I? It doesn't mention Eve. It's as if she never existed.'

'You want to know about your mother,' I said.

She nodded and looked at me from behind the dark lenses, but did not move from her position on the walkway.

'I don't want to tell you in here,' I said.

'I promise I'll not do anything stupid.'

'I still don't want to tell you in here.'

'The Fords said that she died soon after I was born. You confirmed that.'

'It wasn't long, no.'

'Was it suicide?'

I said nothing.

'I believe she killed herself. Women always try to do that with some kind of dignity. It's only men who choose disgusting ways to go. I'll not be shocked.'

I stared down at the stream which ran through a channel

across the floor of the enclosure. Once, in a forest in the north, I had diverted a stream so that it fell through a fissure in a slate outcrop and then coursed across a path which I decorated with shallow stepping-stones quarried in another country. For most visitors everything but the placement of the stones was natural. They recognised neither the artifice of the tiny waterfall nor that the stones were foreign. For me, the piece had something to do with trespass.

'Was it sleeping pills?'

I opened my hands as if I were pleading. I was not sure what to tell her.

'Gas?'

'Yes.'

'Gas?' she repeated, emphasising the word to show she needed confirmation.

'That's how she did it.'

'Were you there? Was *I* there?'

'Look, it was all a long time ago. I try not to think about it. She committed suicide because she was a depressive. I don't mean that loosely; I mean clinically. You have no need to know the details.'

'Don't you think I deserve to be told?'

'It won't solve anything. You gain nothing by knowing.'

'Tell me,' she demanded.

'Somewhere else.'

'Why not here?'

'Because I need to be outside, Grace.'

'My name's Judith. It was Grace when you gave me away.'

'Right. But for God's sake take off those glasses. If I have to tell you, at least let me see your eyes while I'm doing it.'

She followed me through the exit curtain and out onto a broad sweep of pathway. I walked past several of the animal houses, determined not to stop until we reached somewhere quiet. The zoo reeked of fresh dung and disinfected straw, and parties of children clutching school notebooks seemed to have taken over every viewing point.

Eventually we came to a wildfowl pond with empty seats overlooking it. We sat down side by side. Judith crossed her legs so that the split in her skirt widened, and I could see the underside of her thigh. There was a large bruise discolouring it. I wanted to tell her to cover up. She held her glasses in her lap and turned them over every few seconds. I watched them catch the sun so that it seemed reflected in dark ice.

'She was depressive,' Judith repeated.

'Yes.'

'She was morbid and anxious all the time?'

'Eventually. At first there were times when she was optimistic and ebullient, but gradually those became less and less frequent. After you were born it got worse. She cut herself off from everyone. She was worse than neurotic. I begged her to see a doctor; she told me she had, and that she was on medication, but she was lying. I wasn't to know that. Eventually she just took the opportunity when it was there.'

'And what did she do?'

I had worked out my story in advance.

'I had a chance of a commission,' I said. 'Those were early days, and we didn't have any money to speak of, so I went after every opportunity. I left Eve alone with you. It was hours before I got back.'

A baboon or monkey began to scream somewhere behind us. The noise snagged the air and Judith had to raise her voice to be heard.

'You found her?'

'Yes. After we said goodbye she closed the windows and plastered adhesive tape across the cracks. Then she turned the gas taps on to full. It was only a small flat, with one bedroom and a living room. It can't have taken long.'

'Where was I?'

'Safe. There was a tiny cubbyhole we used as a larder. It had a small window. Eve cleared a space on the floor and opened the window as wide as it would go. Then she put you in your carrycot and left it on the floor. She closed the door tight and sealed it with tape. She must have wanted you to be found straight away, because she wrote a message on a piece of paper with felt-tip pen and fastened it to the door.'

'What did it say?'

'To open that door first because you were behind it.'

The cries were cut off suddenly, but for some time the air still vibrated with their urgency.

'And when you came back?'

When I had closed the front door of the house I took my key out of my pocket and climbed the gloomy flights of stairs until I neared the top flat. I knew something was wrong before I reached the last step. I was seized by panic and excitement. The landing smelled of suffocation. I stood in front of the locked door fingering the key while my nostrils filled, and I strained my hearing until I could either detect, or imagine I detected, the sound of gas hissing from taps opened to the limit.

'She'd pushed a rug under the front door but gas had still seeped out onto the landing,' I told Judith. 'I remember searching frantically for my key, praying that she hadn't closed the bolt on the inside. For a moment I thought she had, but it was the door jamming on a rug. I pushed hard and it opened just enough for me to get through the gap. The room was thick with gas.'

My head began to swim as soon as I stepped into the room. I retreated onto the landing. Beside me was a sash window. Pads of moss had forced the hardened putty away from the glass on the outside, and for a few dislocating moments I wanted to avoid all responsibility and do nothing but study their shape and texture. But I opened the window, pressed a handkerchief to my mouth, and walked back into the room.

'The gas was so strong it made me reel,' I went on. 'The cooker stood just inside the door. There was no flame but all the controls were pointing to maximum and gas was flooding out. I turned them off and opened the windows. And I opened the door to the larder, where you'd been left. By then I was sick and dizzy and almost passing out. But I could still hear hissing. The fire was an old one, without thermocouples. Its valve was open as well. I had to get down on my knees to shut the control, and when I stood up the entire room was tilting and yawing.'

'Where was she?'

'In the bedroom. The door had been left partly open but the view was still blocked and I could only see her feet on the bed. They were bare.'

'She was dead?'

'I didn't know that. I could see a pair of shoes on the floor. Eve had placed them exactly as she always left them before going to bed. I walked to the door and pushed it further. She was lying on the bed with her eyes closed. She didn't look dead. I thought she was unconscious but still alive.'

'But she wasn't.'

'The gas had made her look as if she could be – her skin was healthy and pink as if she was just pretending. I saw that she wasn't breathing but I was certain that she still had a chance. The mattress springs had gone and she was sunk too far into it for me to be able to do the kiss of life properly, so I dragged her onto the floor. I remember the odd, heavy thump when her heels hit the floorboards. She'd taken the rug from the bedroom to wedge behind the front door.'

Eve had fallen to the floor with her arms and legs spread a little and her face flushed with false excitement. I had leaned across her like a seducer, a vampire over its prey. I knew if I touched her mouth it would taste of the grave.

'Her lips were cool, not cold, but there was no response. I don't know how long I worked on her. Several minutes, maybe.'

'And me?'

'You were asleep, and breathing steadily and deeply. I knew you were going to be all right.'

'And after a while you gave up.'

'No. We were too poor to own a phone so I ran downstairs to some people on the first floor because I knew they had one. And I remembered I'd seen the man go out a few times wearing a St John's Ambulance uniform. He ran back upstairs with me while his wife dialled 999. He took a look at you and said you would be fine, and then he tried to resuscitate Eve. There was no sign of life. The police and ambulance arrived within a few minutes. They took Eve out on a stretcher, even though they must have realised there was little hope. You were carried out in someone's arms.'

'Yours?'

'They wouldn't let me. A police car drove in front with its blue light flashing and its siren blaring. They put me in the car that followed. They were interviewing me before I knew for certain that Eve was dead.'

'Who told you?'

'A doctor. He said they'd fought for her for as long as they could. The same doctor told me that you'd hardly been affected. Your mother must have sealed that door as tight as a hold.'

'I can't imagine what you must have felt.'

'It was all a long time ago. This is the first time I've talked about it—' I stopped, unwilling to go further.

'When did you bring me back from hospital?'

'They kept you overnight; that's all. But neither Eve nor I had parents or relatives. The woman on the first floor insisted on looking after you for days. To be honest, I was pleased that she did.'

'Was there a suicide note?'

'No.'

'She didn't want to leave any last message?'

I said nothing.

'Well?'

'I told you that Eve was a depressive. At times she was far from rational. She probably killed herself on a stupid impulse. She wouldn't have thought about the real implications of what she was doing, let alone about writing a letter.'

'But she thought about me.'

'Not too clearly, otherwise she wouldn't have endangered you as she did.'

Judith hesitated, then nodded.

The farewell letter had been left beside the bed. I picked it up and hid it between the pages of one of the few books that we possessed. It was an art book.

When the police asked me I told them I had found no note. They asked if I was absolutely sure, because most suicides left a statement behind them. Of course I was sure, I answered; I wouldn't have overlooked something like that.

Afterwards, when I was on my own, I returned to the book. I opened it gingerly, as if it were a rare codex, and took the letter from where it had lain pressed between the pages.

I had to gather my courage to read it. When I did, I found that it was neither justification nor excuse, but only a list of instructions on how to look after Grace, ending with a plea that I should always be there if she needed me. I had feared that Eve would blame me for her own suicide, but there were no accusations. Neither was there any mention of my affair with Angie.

'Is mother buried? Can I see her grave?'

'I scattered her ashes in the garden behind the crematorium. There was nowhere else to put them. Neither of us had homes we could go back to. We were both orphans by then.'

I looked at Judith. There was a sheen across her eyes. I did not know whether or not she was about to cry, so I quickly looked away. Ducks traced liquid arrows across the pond.

'The house quoted on my birth certificate,' she said. 'Was that where it happened?'

'Yes.'

'It's all been rebuilt. There's nothing left. And there's nothing left of her except me.'

'You and a few certificates in registries. In the end that's what happens to most people. We're just entries in archives.'

'But most of us are remembered, at least for a generation or two. That hasn't happened to her. That article didn't mention her and it didn't mention me.'

No, I thought, it didn't; only one article mentioned Eve and Grace. It had been in a long-ago publication called *Art and Artists,* and I had spent much of my life tracking down copies and destroying them.

'There's a reason for that,' I said.

'And?'

'Lillian doesn't know about either of you.'

'You haven't told her?'

I could not answer.

'Is this the first time you've talked about the suicide since it happened? How long have you been together? Twenty years? More?'

'Listen, I don't have to justify myself to you. You have nothing to do with my life, and I have nothing to do with yours.'

'How can you say that?'

'Easily. We're linked by the most tenuous bonds of all, and they're genetic. We have nothing else in common. I thought you'd have understood that by now. I've told you what you want to know. I hope you feel satisfied. But now I want us to walk away and never see or hear from each other again. This has been an extraordinary event in our lives, but it's one I want to forget if I can. I don't want you either as a daughter or a friend.'

'And despite all that you still agreed to meet me. There's something between us, isn't there? Something neither of us can ignore.'

'What thing?'

'I don't know. It's like mercury, try to pick it up and it will only slip away. Don't you feel that, too?'

'I want to leave. That's the only thing I feel.'

'I don't believe you.'

'That makes no difference to me. You're too much trouble, too much of a risk.'

She refused to reply.

'I couldn't have looked after a baby,' I insisted, 'it was sensible to do what I did.'

'You didn't have *anyone* to help?'

'No one. And I knew that to succeed, to even make a living, I would have to travel. It was even possible that I could go somewhere for a few weeks and not come back for a year.'

'You could have had me fostered.'

'Children need stability. A girl needs a mother. That's what I was advised, and that's what I believed. It seemed kinder to sever our connections completely.'

'It was more convenient, you mean.'

'I was promised you would go to a good home. The best.'

'The best? Well, I suppose the Fords tried hard, in their own peculiar way. Didn't you wonder about me?'

'It wasn't long after you were adopted that I went to Japan for a year. It was the best break I ever had. I did work there for a company that still commissions me. Everything back in England seemed a long way away. I began to lead a different life.'

'The kind you live now?'

'It was the beginning, yes.'

'I still can't understand why you don't want to know about me. Aren't you curious at all?'

'I don't want to get involved. As far as I'm concerned it would be like listening to a stranger's life. Whatever your difficulties, I can't solve them. If you have triumphs, I have no wish to share them. I've given you the greatest gift a man can give his child – total independence. Perhaps someday you'll realise how I freed you.'

She made a brief contemptuous noise, part sigh, part hiss. 'You must be really vulnerable.'

'That's cheap psychology.'

'Not cheap; basic.'

I gave a tolerant smile. It was one I often used on students whose enthusiasm exceeded their good sense, but it did not deter Judith.

'Look at the shells you hide inside. Self-regard – *the greatest gift a man can give his child*! The professionalism that you polish up for newspaper interviews. Pretended indifference. Marriage and home. The lies that you told Lillian. Only the vulnerable need so much protection.'

'And you're going to tell me what I'm like inside, are you? Just like an undergraduate who's just been handed her first Freud?'

'I don't know what you're like inside. But I'm certain that somewhere there's a man who wants to know what became of his child. His *only* child, the only one who can carry a part of him into the future.'

'This is getting nowhere.'

'Listen to me. No, say nothing – just listen, and then afterwards we can part and never see each other again, ever.

I'll not haunt you. I'll not write letters to your wife or your other daughter. You'll not see me hanging around your next exhibition. I can vanish back where I came from.'

'You can do that now. I don't need this.'

'*Listen*: there have been times when I've been foolish. When I've behaved badly. Times when others must have thought I was mad.'

'No doubt you had your reasons.'

I stood up with an abruptness which took her by surprise. I tried not to look at her but I was unable to avoid her eyes. They were both vulnerable and questioning, and I wished she had still been wearing her dark glasses.

'I made the wrong choices,' she said. 'We have that in common.'

A momentary terror struck me: did she mean that there was another generation?

'A child?' I asked. My chest was hollow.

'I couldn't bear it. I've had lovers, but it wouldn't be fair to have had a child. It's not something that's going to happen. Not just yet. And perhaps never.'

It was all I needed to be told. 'I have to go,' I said.

'You don't have to, you want to.'

'All right, if you want to pick words, I think it's wise if I leave. Now.'

She stood up to face me. 'Tell me one more thing before you do.'

I made great play of checking that I had left nothing behind on the bench.

'Why didn't you and Lillian have children of your own?'

'That has nothing to do with you.'

'They would have been my brothers and sisters. I'd like to know why they don't exist. Can't Lillian have children?'

'No.'

'Was that disappointing?'

'We knew it before we married. That's why we adopted Claire as soon as we were able to.'

'You got rich so soon?'

'We're still not rich. But we became secure quite quickly. It was the right time to adopt. Until then it wouldn't have been good for a child.'

'Obviously not. I'm the evidence for that.'

I told myself I should say no more, that this was the point at which I could simply turn and walk away, but Judith was determined not to let me go so easily.

'I share a house with a man,' she said.

There was a twinge of relief or resentment, I did not know which.

'It's a matter of convenience,' she explained. 'He was the one who bought the newspaper; the one with the article. If it hadn't been for him, I would never have seen it, never have read it. I owe him a lot in all kinds of ways. But it would be good to have someone else. Someone else to turn to.'

'And that was another reason why you wanted to see me?'

'No. Yes. But I haven't found what I wanted.'

I shrugged, not knowing what to say.

'It was irrational of me to think you might be interested. I see that now. As you said, it has nothing to do with you. Apart from anything else, I've been an adult for a long time. I should be able to sort out my own problems without recourse to a parent.'

'That's right.'

She nodded like an innocent forced into acknowledgment of a guilt.

'And now I really do have to go,' I said.

'So this is goodbye?'

I saw her register my momentary hesitation; perhaps her eyes widened in that instant.

'I think it's best,' I said.

'Are you glad I made contact?'

I had to leave now or become further entangled. A clean break was the best break of all.

'No,' I said abruptly, and then I turned and walked away.

Like a man on the run I wanted to sprint for the gates, but I also wanted to look back and fix Judith's image in my memory for one last time. I paced my strides to be rapid but without panic, and made myself look straight ahead. Around me the zoo's perspectives shifted, as in an optical illusion. It seemed that the massive walls and high cages became less substantial, that their depth shrank so that they were as unreal as stage backdrops. Soon I began to notice that my breathing was fast and shallow.

I glanced at my reflection in a kiosk mirror. I had shed my affluence and confidence. The man who stared back was older than his years; revelation dragged so heavily at his face that I wanted to hide.

The pavilion for nocturnal animals was nearby. I chose it as a refuge and entered it quickly, my eyes downcast as I descended the steps into its underground bunkers.

Blackness hunched in the corners of the long rooms and angled corridors. In the dim illumination from the display cases I saw my hands turn a cold reptilian green.

I traced a slow, loitering, obsessive's path around the exhibits. Behind their glass, in facsimiles of night, termites gorged on felled wood and armadillos nosed through gifts of leaves dropped into their cases as if by a divine hand. I glanced at them but kept my concentration on the people shuffling around me through the artificial night. At a distance they were beyond identification; their jade faces were blurred with shadow and their voices squeezed out of true. Only when they came nearer did they become distinctive. All the time I expected Judith to emerge from the mossy darkness and torment me with bitter, senseless questions about my life.

I stopped in the labyrinth for a long time before I felt safe, and when I returned to the outside world it was awash with a steely light that hurt the eyes.

Lillian was waiting for me when I returned home. 'A good day?' she asked.

'Frustrating.'

She looked at me questioningly. I half-turned away from her and busied myself emptying my pockets of keys, a wallet, and small change. We always kept some money in a metal ashtray. I tilted my hand over it and the coins clattered like a ransom as they fell.

'I spent some time at the zoo,' I said. 'I thought I might pick up a few ideas in the nocturnal section.'

'And did you?'

'No. It was too depressing. The visitors were like dead people on their way to the Styx.'

'That's rather fanciful,' Lillian murmured.

I shrugged. 'I said it was frustrating.'

'Weren't you able to make any progress at all?'

I shook my head. 'Maybe I need a break. What do you think? Maybe it would help if I just stopped brooding about the Peermain wood.'

'It's possible. But you said you would work tonight.'

'I'd just be wasting time; I don't have a concept to work on. Let's go somewhere together instead. A restaurant? The cinema? We might even be able to get theatre tickets. Where would you like to go?'

'Jamie, I have reports to read and papers to assess.'

'I know. Do them tomorrow.'

'I shouldn't. Some of us can't afford to be too late with our work.'

I stood up, walked across the room, and embraced her.

'Persuader,' she said.

'Let's go. Anywhere you want.'

She smiled and pretended to escape, but I held her more tightly and murmured in her ear. We were like people who had just become lovers.

'I'll book a table at one of our restaurants,' I said. 'We'll drink enough wine to make us giddy. And when we get back here we'll go straight to bed, only half-undressed, and do things that we might never have done before.'

'I can't imagine what they might be,' she laughed, 'I thought we'd covered all the variations.'

Later that night, lying beside Lillian in the dishevelled gloom with a clock's bright numbers counting noiselessly beside us, I thought again about the zoo, and imagined that as I skulked within its cellars Judith was walking above me. I dreamed that the bunker roof turned magically into a one-way glass impenetrable by sunlight, and I saw myself clutched within a green-flecked darkness, staring up through the glass to where my abandoned daughter strode, the sun catching her hair, her black skirt opening like a page part-lifted on an unread book. The white swell of her bruised thigh signalled her maturity, but also reminded me of the life I had led with her mother.

In the very dead of night, as alert as I had ever been, I left Lillian in a deep, contented sleep and walked downstairs in bare feet to my desk.

I found the cheque book, opened it, and almost returned it to the drawer. The impulse rolled over my hesitation. I wrote out a cheque but left the stub blank.

Then, seized by the need to complete my task as soon as I could, I addressed an envelope to Judith, stamped it, sealed the cheque inside without any accompanying note, and hid it. In the morning I would post it, and then I would think no more of her. She would be wiped from my life forever.

It was only when I got back into bed that I realised I had

hidden Judith's cheque, just as I had hidden her mother's suicide note, between the pages of a book on art.

Lillian murmured, three-quarters asleep, and moved the warm curve of her body towards mine. I put one arm around her, encompassing her back, hips, and the crook of her legs within my own. The smell and texture of her hair was in my nostrils. At that moment I loved her more than I had ever done. My heart was tender with her presence, chilled by the possibility of loss. Judith Ford was not only a ghost from my own past, she was a danger to my happiness, a threat to my marriage.

As I lay there in the gloom I remembered how, just after we had first met, Lillian had taken me to a performance of *Hamlet*. Single-mindedness about painting and sculpture had driven me to ignore the theatre and literature, and she was convinced that I should have some knowledge of classics from the other arts. In the first act an unexpected sense of fatalism raced through me. Hamlet tells Horatio that because of one particular fault, the stamp of one defect, men become corrupt; ultimately, no matter what, they will be condemned.

Lillian heard nothing but the verse, but I brooded on my own particular fault. My defect was not a failing of my personality, but the nature of youth. It had been beyond my control; I was not responsible. I was determined not to let it drag down the remainder of my life.

After Eve's death I had only sought partners who would not impinge on my ambition. I wanted to be indifferent to others, to live a life uncluttered by emotion. The complexities of form and materials, the uncertainties of commissions and working space, were enough for me. My relationships with other people had to be simple, undemanding, temporary.

Within a few weeks of meeting Lillian my ideas had changed. Dazed by my own happiness and good fortune, I could have no interest in any other woman. Soon I began to reason that I had misunderstood my own needs. I was not, after all, the kind of artist who would accumulate affair after affair, none of them central, as his life progressed. Instead I needed stability; it was even possible that I would thrive on love. Before Lillian I had never suspected this might be true.

It was not just attraction, not just a kind of shared enthusiasm that bound us to each other. Quite early in our relationship, and long before we had slept together, Lillian and I discussed my future. I had not thought of my career as being manageable, or even controllable; to me it seemed to be nothing but a product of reputation and chance. It was Lillian who persuaded me that an ascent could be plotted as effectively as a military operation. She taught me how to channel my ambition and broaden my appeal. At the same meeting I almost told her the truth about my past. Within a few more days the truth was no longer possible. We sailed a strong current, and had already been swept beyond that shoal.

Within six months of that discussion I had left my old agency and signed up with a more powerful one. Schooled by Lillian, and backed by her wider knowledge, I was able to talk with cool precision about the work of other artists, including writers, while remaining tantalisingly enigmatic about my own. I had never lacked confidence in my sculpture, but I had professed to despise certain buyers and patrons because I secretly feared that they would dismiss it or, worse, ignore it. Within a year we had begun to count these people as our friends.

Not that I was a completely changed man. I still had periods of sullen doubt, sometimes of indiscriminate anger. Lillian tolerated these and talked me through them. I knew that she considered my moods to be immature, but that they were necessary companions to my creativity. If I was bad-tempered to her, or annoyed with Claire, she tended to me like an older sister. At the rare times when I doubted myself she was always there to restore my confidence. I had even decided that, if ever I had an affair, Lillian would be tolerant of that, too. She would reason that it was my latent immaturity taking another form, and she would be so confident of herself that she could demand its end and know that I would comply.

I had been faithful to Lillian since the day that we met. But although she would forgive me an affair, she would never forgive a lie that had lasted the length of our life together.

3

'Judith?'

'Yes?'

'It's Jamie McGoldrick.'

A pause, and then she said, 'I thought I recognised the voice.'

'I sent you a cheque. Last week.'

'Yes.'

'It hasn't been cashed.'

'No.'

I imagined her tearing it up, as I had torn up her letter; as, many years ago, I had torn up her mother's. 'Have you still got it?' I asked.

'You can have it back if you want.'

'Of course I don't. It's for you. I just wanted to make sure you had it.'

'I've got it all right. The trouble is I don't know if I should feel grateful or insulted.'

'Just cash it.'

'Will that make you feel better? A thousand pounds is enough to ease your conscience?'

'It's money that I can afford and that you need. Don't make problems where there are none. I want you to have it.'

'Why? You said I meant nothing to you.'

'Judith, just take the cheque and put it in your bank, all right?'

'Alex needs some materials.'

'What?'

'I could buy him some. Board, paper, paint.'

'Who's Alex?'

'It's his house. I live here. I told you.'

'The house needs work done on it; is that what you mean?'

'No, he's a *painter*. That's why he read the article about you. He always reads articles like that. He says it keeps him up to date.'

'He's an artist?'

'He says you won't have heard of him. He hasn't had much success yet, but he will. I'm sure he will.'

'Listen, Judith, the money's for you, not for your friend Alex.'

'You said nothing about how it should be spent.'

'No, but I assumed you would spend it usefully.'

'It would be useful to buy Alex what he needs.'

'No, it would be useful for you to look after yourself. Buy some new clothes. Or if you have enough clothes, treat yourself to a short holiday. Or spend it on food or books or CDs.'

'You really want me to spend it like that?'

'Of course I do.'

There was a long pause.

'All right. Maybe I could think of a few things.'

'Good,' I said, relieved.

'But I can't accept the cheque. It's too much.'

'I didn't mean you should spend it all at once.'

'Mr McGoldrick, what do you want me to feel about this? That I'm accepting your charity?'

'No, of course not.'

'You want me to accept it as a gift, right? A present from you to me?'

'I suppose so. Yes.'

'Then you should see where your money goes.'

'I'll trust you to make the right choices.'

'That's not the point. You should see what you're paying for. And besides, I'll need your advice.'

I did not answer.

'It seems that you're a well-connected man. You know a lot of people – artists, businessmen, critics, gallery owners, professors.'

'I come into contact with them. That doesn't mean I'm friends with them all.'

'Alex knows a few college lecturers and a lot of students. That's about all. But I'm sure he'll break into your kind of world before too long. I'd like to know more about it.'

'About the art world? All you can do is go to exhibitions and read the right magazines.'

'No, I *want* to know more about it. Alex needs a partner who can talk to him on more equal terms. That's why I need someone to give me an insider's view. I don't want to rely on what the papers say or what gets shown on television. I want to know what's really important, what's fashionable, what can be dismissed. I need a guide.'

'There are plenty of people who could be your guide.'

'Yes,' she said, as crisply as a lawyer scoring a point, 'but none of them has given me money.'

I did not want to meet again at the station. Like a traitor, I believed it would be prudent to change our rendezvous, so we eventually agreed to meet at a particular corner of a busy square. Tentative sunlight gave a sheen to the fountains and blanched the paving, and the air was filled with the flap of pigeons' wings and the continuous hiss of water.

Judith had arrived before me and taken a seat on a

concrete bench at the edge of the square. She was wearing jeans that were ripped across one knee and a black leather jacket that was several years old. Her hair had been brushed back from her face, emphasising the prominence of the cheekbones.

I sat beside her. Pigeons with eyes like cheap jewellery strutted towards our feet and then waddled away disappointed.

'Hold out your hand,' she said.

I was puzzled.

'Go on,' she insisted.

I extended my palm and she dropped a dozen small green fragments of paper into it. My cheque. She had torn it so methodically that it was well beyond recovery.

'There's a bin over there,' she said.

Heat flared inside me. I had spent years working towards affluence, and hated to see senseless destruction. My feelings must have been evident for Judith touched me lightly on the shoulder to placate me. The fact of her touch was like a muffled shock. I felt my muscles tense around the point of contact.

'I couldn't take it off you,' she said; 'really I couldn't.'

'You brought me here under false pretences.'

'I meant what I said. If you want to help me then I'm grateful, but a cheque like that is either an extravagance or an insult. It's too much for a stranger. But at forty pounds a year, it's nothing for a daughter. Smaller things would mean more to me. A cheque is like a pay-off. A bribe.'

She was right, but I did not know how alert she was to my motivations.

'How small? If I bought you anything I wouldn't use my credit card.'

'Why not? Are you worried that Lillian will read your statement?'

She was right. A cheque, even a large one, could be disguised; an itemised print-out of stores would be impossible. I looked in my wallet. I had enough notes; and if not, there were cash machines all over town.

'Try being precise about what you want,' I said.

Her answer came without hesitation. Expectation was coiled within each sentence.

'Something to remember you by. Something distinctive that will always remind me of you. A piece of music, perhaps, or a favourite book. I couldn't ask you for something that you'd made.'

'No you couldn't. Because, just like you couldn't afford to buy one, I couldn't afford to give one away.'

'Not many people find out that their father is famous. And not just in this country, either. *World* famous.'

I looked across the square. Japanese tourists were paying to photograph two girls dressed in the glamorised punk clothing of twenty years ago. They were refugees from a generation which had vanished while my daughter was still at primary school.

Judith misunderstood my silence. 'I didn't think modesty was one of your qualities,' she said. As she spoke a flight of pigeons took off from the paving stones. They made a tight wheel above our heads and landed unconcerned near to their take-off point.

Conceit made me rash.

'I had a collection of my work published two years ago. The specialist bookshops and the galleries stock copies. Just as long as you don't expect me to sign one.'

'Haven't you got your own?'

'Lillian has them counted.'

She nodded her sympathy. 'Alex says that art books are too expensive.'

'He's right.'

As a student I had had to rely on the overused books in

the college library, although once or twice I had succeeded in stealing a volume from a shop. The long coat which I had habitually sported, even in summer, had proved a godsend in such matters. Now, as a form of penance, I visited those same shops to buy books which I did not need.

'The Americans have some of your smaller pieces,' Judith said. 'The Museum of Modern Art—'

'Contemporary Art. It's in Los Angeles. And the Hirshorn in Washington.'

'Do you have anything on show in town?'

I nodded. 'There's a small wooden sculpture at—'

She interrupted. 'Let's go there. We can walk. There's a bookshop as well.'

For several seconds I did not realise how fully she had anticipated me. Neither did I appreciate that her last sentence was not a query but a statement.

'It would take twenty or thirty minutes,' I warned.

'That's not a problem. I feel like walking today. Shall we go?'

'There's an art bookshop closer than that. I know people at the gallery.'

'And they'll think I'm your mistress? That's exciting. Don't all artists have lovers? Wouldn't your friends be intrigued by me; wouldn't they think you ever-so-mysterious, bringing along a young woman whom no one knew and no one had ever seen before?'

'If we meet anyone,' I said firmly, 'you're a student, that's all. You recognised me and we got into conversation. We have nothing, *nothing* to do with each other. And if anyone remarks how we look like each other, deny it.'

Her smile was mocking and broad. 'Deny the truth? I do love pretence.'

'Just do as I say. Please.'

'Of course. But it's not likely we'll meet anyone.'

As we followed the wide pavements Judith began to

ask me questions, not about my life or work, but about aspects of the art world which she thought could be easily explained. Most of these were easy (what did I know about Barbara Hepworth, Robert Smithson?), but sometimes I was puzzled. I spent a while ruminating on an artist named Rudd until I realised that her memory was at fault and she meant Donald Judd. She also asked how exhibitions were organised, whether or not critical opinion affected sales prices, and exactly how organisations chose the artists that they commissioned. I formed the impression that not only was she concerned about Alex's lack of progress, but also that she had memorised names she had read in art magazines so that she could confront me with them.

All the time, as we walked, I was aware of the statues of soldiers and politicians that had been placed every few hundred yards along our path. This was ceremonial art, slavishly representational; sculpture that was as naturalistic and lifeless as a waxwork.

When we neared the river Judith recalled that when she had been about thirteen she had walked this very path at dusk, and that the water had been higher than she had ever seen it.

'I stopped to look over the parapet,' she said. 'All I had to do was stretch out my hand and I could have touched the surface with my fingertips.'

I thought this an exaggeration. 'I've never heard of the river being so swollen,' I said.

'It's true. If there had been a tiny breach in the wall water would have poured into the city. Everything seemed poised; nothing was certain. I've had the feeling since, but not about anything as easily imagined as a flood. There are times when I know I'm on the edge of something, something hardly recognisable, but unstoppable. I have that feeling now, Jamie. I have it about you.'

'You should forget it. We're not going to flood each

other's lives. I've made that clear from the first time we spoke.'

As soon as we entered the gallery I led Judith towards the far room where one of my sculptures was on show. To reach it we had to pass through displays of work from Matisse onward, but I scarcely noticed the exhibits; instead I scanned the people around us, worried that a familiar face might confront us without warning.

'Giacometti,' Judith said with the precision of someone who has learned a few foreign words but is not certain of their actual meaning. 'That's a Brancusi head over there. Those are Rauschenbergs.'

'You've been here before.'

'A few months ago. I memorised the names.'

'Your friend brought you?'

'Alex doesn't care for abstracts. He spends most of his time looking at figurative work. Old Masters, that kind of thing.'

It was a long time since I had heard the phrase *Old Masters*. Nowadays only amateurs used it.

Judith continued. 'He showed me how religious paintings have secret codes built into them – peacocks mean resurrection; did you know that?'

'Probably.'

'And he has a particular liking for Goya.'

'He's not an Old Master.'

'Isn't he? There – do you see what I mean? I need to find out that sort of thing. As for Goya, well, some of his paintings are beautiful, but others turn my stomach. Dead babies. Atrocity victims. Executed soldiers.'

'*The Disasters Of War*? They're etchings.'

'Whatever. Alex says Goya is one of the few painters who is honest about suffering. That's one of his yardsticks – the depiction of suffering.'

'Your Alex must be harsh judge. And a limited one.'

'He says he's right.'

'No doubt. And had he heard about me? Before he read the article?'

'He joked about you.'

'Joked?'

'Alex knows all about my past. He said that with a name like McGoldrick you must be a relative. When he saw your photograph he pointed to it and said "He looks so much like you it could be your uncle". It was one of those moments when everything begins to change. We began to realise exactly who you were.'

The more I heard about Alex the less I trusted him, but I could think of no means of buying his silence.

I slowed at the entrance to the last gallery before the new exhibition rooms. Pale light radiated through a high glass canopy, soothing the room until it was broken by edgily dark constructions arranged on the parquet floor. Here were pieces of metal, concrete and plastic, each of them positioned for the best effect. Near the far corner a man and a woman in well-dressed middle age pondered my exhibit. It was a bulbous tree-trunk, seven feet high, stripped of its bark and varnished to a rich copper brown.

'I'm in here,' I said to Judith, keeping my voice down.

'I haven't seen these before.'

'They're all recent acquisitions. Mine is the wooden piece.'

She inclined her head towards the trunk and I gave a tiny nod of agreement. I had no wish to hear what was said about my work, and did not want to approach the couple, but Judith tugged at my sleeve like a demanding child and I found myself sauntering across the floor towards my own sculpture.

The man consulted the printed sheet he held in one hand. '*Beech Trunk; Jamie McGoldrick,*' he said in a spirit of cool inquiry. Then, alert to our presence, he pitched his voice to be as knowing as an expert's.

This was one of McGoldrick's small, transportable works, he continued. Generally the artist preferred his work to be viewed in contexts other than galleries or museums. His sculpture could be seen in many countries, including Japan, Australia, Switzerland and the USA. He always insisted on visiting sites and making a careful study of them before he began to think about the shape, texture and colour of the piece that could occupy the chosen space. Although a minority of his works had been created to decay, the bulk of his output was permanent, albeit not necessarily easily accessible. Recently McGoldrick had received a major commission to create a site-specific sculpture for the English headquarters of an international Japanese electronics company. It seemed, therefore, that one of Britain's major contemporary artists would at last be able to create a large permanent work that could be viewed in his own country.

While the man talked the woman made small, rapid gestures with her hands, as if she wished to demonstrate the trunk's tactile qualities. Her face had the sharp angularity of the stylishly underfed.

When her companion stopped talking the woman began to muse on the geometry of the piece, using the word *mass* as if this was, in itself, a critical insight. She speculated that the curvature hinted at a meaning which the title refused to make explicit. And she indicated minuscule tattoo-like indentations on parts of the surface; surely this must mean something?

We stood nearby but said nothing. They did not acknowledge us and finally moved away through the door to the new exhibition. I could hear the man's voice begin to drone like a distant bee.

'How could you listen to them without saying anything?' Judith asked.

'Did you see that leaflet in his hand? It's a quick guide to the recent acquisitions. You can pick it up at the information desk. He was paraphrasing it; he had nothing original to say. And as for his wife, if that's who she was, she thought this must weigh as much as the original trunk.'

'It doesn't?'

'It's hollowed out so that two men can lift it easily. It was a fallen beech that I was able to buy. I was also able to direct how it should be chainsawed.'

'Is it just a game, then?'

'A serious game. Some postmodern sculpture plays with the reliability of the senses. This looks as if it would take a fork-lift truck to get it into position, but it can be pushed where you want it to go without real difficulty. It's a kind of comment on how appearance and reality may not be the same thing.'

'Does it say that on the leaflet?'

'No. But people think it's a solid object. They don't see that it's the surface that matters. Do you see those marks that she said were like tattoos? They're tracks; the burrows of tiny beetles that lived beneath the bark. The patterning isn't mine, it's theirs.'

Although I did not confess it, the visitors' comments had filled me with a quiet satisfaction. No doubt others would see a correspondence with labyrinths, or the cup-and-ring symbols cut into megaliths; perhaps the more academic would speculate on meaning as recondite as any symbol ever placed between glass sheets by Duchamp. I always enjoy puzzlement in others.

'People will look at it in different ways,' Judith said. 'It reminded that woman of something else. Something she couldn't quite identify.'

'Good,' I said succinctly.

'It reminds me of something too.'

I was determined not to ask her. 'Have you seen enough?'

'Something *I* can't identify either.'

'I'll take you to the bookshop.'

'Can't we spend more time here?'

'I'd rather not. Come on, the bookshop is this way, at the far side of the new exhibits.'

The new exhibition was a collection of automata. A paint gun irregularly sprayed a huge board so that its whiteness was irrevocably vandalised by dribbling swathes of black. A suspended piano suddenly tilted so that its hammers and wires slipped forward as if the instrument had been eviscerated, and the gallery echoed with a discordant crash. Rectangular metal trays holding long pools of mercury, like the blades of ancient swords, juddered erratically and made the mercury slither with the oily grace of snakes.

I felt a surge of justification. My own sculpture was sometimes attacked; it was inaccessible, or mandarin, or merely flippant. But I was satisfied with its validity and its permanence. In a hundred years' time, five hundred, much of my art would still be there, still be on show, still able to give pleasure and intrigue and perhaps even annoyance to those who visited it. That was why I was an important artist, and that was why I was becoming more and more sharply aware that I would have to produce something on the Peermain estate that would be both worthy of my talents, and justify them.

When we reached the shop I found that there was only one copy of my book left on the shelves. It was sealed in a cellophane wrapper with a price sticker fastened to the surface. On the front cover of the jacket was a photograph of a line of bronze panels fixed into slits I had had cut into rounded granite boulders; commentators had claimed they could have been inspired by Roman shields, neolithic avenues, or lizard fins. I had never responded to any of these suggestions.

'This is the only copy they have,' I murmured. I did not want anyone else in the shop to identify me.

'I'll enjoy opening it,' Judith answered.

'But not here. Outside.'

I paid at the counter, hoping that the assistant would not compare the photograph on the back cover with my own face, but if she had seen any likeness she kept it to herself.

'We'll leave now,' I told Judith; 'you've got what you came for.'

We walked towards the doors. The space in front of them was thronged with visitors entering and leaving the gallery. I had to elbow past them to make my way out. Once outside I began to descend the broad steps, but when I turned to speak to Judith I found she was not there.

For a few moments I was perplexed. I looked round to see if somehow she had slipped ahead of me, but she had not. I stood motionless with the book in my hand. Visitors streamed up and down the steps on either side of me. Eventually I decided I would have to go back into the building, and at that moment Judith came out of the doors and walked down the steps.

'Was there a problem?' I asked as we reached the pavement together.

There was a satisfied smirk on her face.

'Well?'

'As we were leaving the bookshop that couple came in – the ones who'd been looking at your beech trunk. Didn't you see them? I couldn't resist telling them who you are. They were astonished. I loved seeing the expression on their faces. They'll know you next time.'

'That was a stupid thing to do,' I complained. 'I don't want to hear any of their brainless questions.'

Without thinking I took hold of Judith's elbow to hurry her along. She walked with me like a willing captive.

'Where are we going?'

'There's a small park at the rear of the building. It's usually quiet. We'll go there.'

The cherry trees along the street were losing their blossom, and the slipstream from passing cars whirled petals across the flagstones and settled them into broken spirals. I wondered what I was doing, walking the pavement with this castaway from the past who had refused my money but was accepting my gifts, and who was foolish or conceited enough to reveal my identity to other strangers.

And then I told myself that I was indulging not only her, but also my own secret and irrational dreams. And that it was time to call a halt, before things went any further.

We walked to the rear of the gallery, crossed the road, and entered the park. Within the black iron railings there was an expanse of grass with a border of soil planted with cherry trees and rhododendrons. A few green tips of new growth showed in the heavy earth. I brushed fallen pink blooms from the slats of a bench so that we could sit down, and then handed Judith the bag with the book in it.

She took out the book, stared at the front, and then turned it over. The cellophane reflected the sky so my photograph seemed to be sheathed in blind ice.

'Does it describe your life?' she asked.

'It's about my work, not my life. The broad outline is in there – birthplace, art school, fellowships, exhibitions. More than I wanted, really. And Lillian is there as well.'

'But not Eve. And not me.'

'I'm sure you didn't expect to be included.'

'I'm scared to open it.'

'I don't think so.'

Judith took a deep breath and grinned as self-consciously as a student waiting to open examination results. Then she found a corner to the wrapping, lifted it and pulled. The cellophane ripped easily and in a moment she had stripped it away entirely.

'I love the smell of new paper,' she said, opening the volume as if it were a rare treasure.

At first I pretended to be more interested in the park, but soon I was sneaking a view of the pages as she turned them.

'There's a photograph of the two of you,' Judith said.

The shadows and grain of the print displayed a glossy, pearly assurance. Lillian and I, three years younger, no less confident, looked out of the page like ambassadors from our own lives.

I remembered that the session had lasted almost an entire afternoon. A week later we had sat with the photographer and editor sifting through more than sixty contact prints. Eventually Lillian had made the decision. The best image looked, she said, like a brass-rubbing of success. She was only half-joking.

'It was right that the book should include Lillian,' I told Judith.

'But it doesn't include my mother,' she repeated, 'and it doesn't include me. It's as misleading as that newspaper profile.'

'You *know* I couldn't put you in.'

She did not turn the page. 'How did you meet?'

'Lillian? She visited an exhibition. We got talking.'

'Eve.'

I did not answer for a short while. Instead I watched a laborious fat woman with a terrier on the end of a taut lead enter the far corner of the gardens. The cast-iron gate squeaked heavily behind her.

'I can't remember,' I said eventually. 'We were students together. There wasn't one big dramatic moment. It didn't happen like that.'

'You didn't intend to marry?'

'In those days we thought that marriage was reactionary and bourgeois. I changed.'

'And was I an accident?'

'Yes.'

The alteration in her face was barely discernible, and may have been nothing but a variation in the light as sun tried to break through the high clouds.

I tried to console her. 'No one was to blame. You weren't the result of a foolish impulse, or anything like that. We were lovers.'

'Does that mean you loved each other?' she asked abruptly.

I had expected the question. 'Of course we did. We were young. Younger than you are now.'

There was a moment of stillness, and then Judith opened the book. The first illustration showed a sleek needle, reflective as polished chrome, pointing straight upwards into equatorial skies. On the next page was the quotation from Berkeley that had been suggested by Terry Evans.

'What it says about truth being a game. Is that true?'

'I believe so.'

She shrugged and turned over more pages. Here was my stainless steel mirror fixed into a mountainside to catch the midsummer sunrise; my bronze castings of the roots of felled trees, punched into the ground like gigantic rivets; my roc's egg of elegantly shaped white limestone set among red outcrops at the edge of a desert; my grid of black marble spheres, crammed together, as glistening and inky as caviare. Here were my glass pyramids and stone gardens, my geometries and enigmas, my transformations, my apotheoses.

'There are photographs of you making most of these,' Judith commented.

'Those are only a selection. There are hundreds more.

These days it's common to record the making of a piece; in some cases it's all that remains of the work.'

'You build these all on your own?'

'I have helpers.'

'There aren't many shown on the photographs.'

'That's because I'm the artist. They're just assistants.'

'You couldn't make these things without them.'

'They're still just assistants.'

She turned more pages, and looked at me enquiringly. Her fingers rested on a photograph taken in the grounds of the estate. 'These pieces of wood,' she asked.

'They interlock. I would have liked to have made them all from the same tree, but commercially available trees don't grow that big. And of course no one could actually lock them together – they're too cumbersome, too massive.'

'They're like a puzzle that a giant has discarded. What shape would they form?'

'A three-dimensional star; it says in the text.'

'And this? Sand in ice?'

'Desert sand. And not just in ice; in a glacier. I was interested in extremes. At one end of the scale, the essential element of all life, but frozen and inactive; at the other, the ultimate sterile material. When it reaches the glacier snout the matrix will disintegrate and the sand will cascade into the meltwater. That was planned to happen a few years from now, but we've had hot summers and the glaciers are thawing faster than expected. I like some pieces to have a kind of self-destructive dynamism. I wanted to sink a cube of ice into the desert, as well; but we couldn't get funding for that.'

'But what you're working on now is permanent?'

'As long-lasting as the Great Wall of China. That's the intention.'

'You much prefer that.'

'Of course. It's impossible to give gravity to a corruptible work.'

'Are there no photographs in here of your new commission? Not even a sketch?'

'There couldn't be. The offer hadn't even been made when the book was printed.'

'You spend a lot of time at the estate?'

I sensed trouble. 'I'm not going to take you, Judith.'

'I wasn't thinking about going with you,' she said, turning a page emphatically, 'I was thinking of going with Alex.'

'You'll not get in. Visits have to be approved.'

'And if we mention your name?'

'You'd better not.'

She smiled to demonstrate that she had been teasing me. 'You know I wouldn't do that. But I do find your actions odd. My mother's body is burned to ash so that nothing exists of her. And you begin to make objects that you expect to last for thousands of years.'

I gave a dismissive laugh. 'There's no connection at all.'

'I can see one.'

'You imagine it, you mean.'

She did not respond.

'I'm interested in shape, colour, pattern, function. Even if there was a link with my own life, I wouldn't explore it. I'm not interested in autobiographical work. Since I left art school I've never done that. I don't think I ever shall.'

She turned over several pages, glancing at each one only cursorily.

'You don't have to sit here,' I said. 'It's yours. Take it home.'

'When you started, were you influenced by Brancusi? Hepworth?'

'For someone who doesn't know much about art, you have a liking for comparison.'

'I don't know much; you must realise by now that I

don't. But I was told you were influenced by Brancusi and Hepworth. And Tatlin. And maybe Rudd.'

'Judd.'

'Right.'

She had listed the names sceptically, like an agnostic counting a rosary. 'Do you know any of their works?' I asked.

'I've been shown one or two.'

'I see. Exactly how much have you told your friend Alex about me?'

She ignored my question and leafed through the pages again. Works I had laboured on for weeks or months flashed and turned like slowly shuffled cards.

'I can see what he means,' she said.

'You haven't answered my question.'

'I confide in Alex. He's a good friend.'

'I've said nothing at all to Lillian. It would have been better if you had been as silent.'

She closed the book, made sure that the jacket sat squarely around it, and placed it back in its bag.

'I can't afford books, let alone expensive art books. Do you really think that Alex wouldn't notice this? Of course I have to talk about you. But you needn't worry; he'll say nothing to anyone.'

'How much are you going to tell him about today?'

'Whatever he wants to know.'

'Tell him nothing.'

'I have to. I rely on him. And he has an income. It may be unpredictable, but it's more than I have. To begin with he paid me for modelling. The house is full of portraits of me.'

'But you must have *some* income.'

'In a way.'

'You mean that you're unemployed?'

'Officially. But I've been a waitress, a secretary, a checkout girl. I've worked in two factories. And I'm a failed actress and dancer, too. I was good at acting; I shouldn't haven given that up so easily. You said you didn't want to know about my life.'

'You needed that money.'

She looked up into the sky, like a child confronted by a difficult question.

'Didn't you?'

'Yes.'

I shook my head despairingly.

'Technically I owe rent to Alex – at least that's what I say on my claim form to the DHSS. Not that Alex would take money from me. He's done everything as well – labouring, teaching, selling satellite TV. He taught at an art college for two years, but gave it up to concentrate on his own work.'

'And you tore up my cheque.'

She looked across the gardens. The old woman was crouching awkwardly as she struggled to unsnap the terrier's lead from its collar. As soon as it was free the dog rushed energetically around the shrubbery and began to bark with a penetrating insistency.

'There must be something you can do,' I protested. I sought for compliments that were not effusive; they needed to sound genuine. 'You're intelligent and personable. You could command a reasonable income, perhaps even a good one.'

'I'm happy where I am. For the moment.'

'Living in someone else's house, and in debt to them?'

'I owe him nothing; we share things. And if Alex earns money then he gives me some.'

'That's too unpredictable.'

'It's all I have.'

'You said you'd made mistakes.'

She was silent.

'When we first met. You said you'd made mistakes.'

'Hasn't everyone?'

'Maybe not the kind that you made.'

'Do you mean Alex?'

'I mean everything. Him included.'

She turned to me quickly, like an animal goaded beyond endurance. I was taken aback by her unrestrained fury.

'Do you want to know about me or not? I don't know where I am with you. And if you think I want you to understand me, then you're wrong.'

She stood up quickly. I could see her body tremble with incoherent passion.

'This relationship is futile,' she said, pronouncing the words as if the very act of speaking was painful. 'We may as well part now and never see each other again. Thank you for the book; you can have it back if you feel it's been a waste of your money.'

I stood up too, but with forced deliberation. 'You do yourself no good with this kind of attitude, Grace.'

'It's *Judith*. For Christ's sake.'

'I'm sorry. Forgive me.'

She shook her head angrily. 'I'll never forgive you. You drove my mother to death and then you abandoned me.'

This time I felt my own anger flare. 'That's a lie. How dare you say that?'

'Because you act like a guilty man. You tell no one about me, not even your wife. At first you don't want to know me, and then you try to buy my silence with money. A thousand pounds! I could make more if I phoned that newspaper and sold them the story.'

'I'm an artist, not an actor. My past has no commercial value.'

'It has no emotional value either, has it? Not for you.'

'You're a selfish woman and there's more than a touch

of bitch in you,' I said as calmly as I could. 'I'm pleased we'll have nothing more to do with each other.'

Her face tightened. She swung the book at my chest so that it hit me across the ribs. I saw the blow coming and did not move. There was a muffled thud but no sensation of hurt; instead the shock of contact jarred Judith's hand. A reflex sprang her fingers apart and the book slipped from them. Like an angel lifting a wounded hero, I caught it before it fell.

'You may not be able to respect me, but try to respect my book,' I said.

Her hand came up to my face. It moved quickly but I could still have avoided it if I had wanted to. A slight pain brushed my cheek hesitantly and without apparent malevolence. Even the noise it made was comfortingly domestic, for the sound was like my own fingers massaging a chin I had not shaved for days.

Judith stepped back, her head turned away, her striking hand clasped within the other as if it had been damaged. I held the book in one hand and put the other up to my cheek.

The terrier hurtled across the flagstones, delighting in its own furious vigour. Within a few seconds it was harrying, worrying at my shoes and ankles.

I tried to step away but it came after me, tiny and demonic, rapidly snapping its vicious little jaws until just as quickly it tired of the sport and scampered back to its owner. As it ran it bounced, proud as any conqueror. She did not even reprimand it.

I looked down at my trouserlegs, which were drenched with frothy saliva, and then I realised that my hand was still pressed against my cheek. I took it away and immediately half of my face began to sting bitterly and severely.

Judith had sat down on the seat furthest away from me.

Her legs were slightly apart and one hand was still cradled within the other.

'What have you done to me?' I asked. My voice trembled like a sail in wind.

'I've scratched your face, that's all.'

'Christ,' I said, shocked.

'I'm not proud of it,' she said aggressively.

I glanced around in panic for a place where I might examine my reflection. Only the windows of the houses on the far side of the gardens offered any hope.

'How bad is it?' I asked.

'You'll not scar.'

'How do you know that?'

'Relax. I know.'

I pressed my hand against the hurt as if I could smother it. When I took it away there were shapeless smudges of blood on my palm.

'Give me the book,' she said. I handed it to her and she placed it on the bench. Then she produced a small hand mirror which she snapped open and held out face upwards. For the first time I noticed that there were wire-thin lines crossing the insides of her wrists. The mirror had two sides, plain and magnifying, and the sky trembled momentarily within the glass. I took the mirror and held it so that I could examine my wound.

Scored down one side of my face were three inflamed vertical marks with drops of blood strung along them like tiny beads. Judith's nails had raked down the cheek and ripped through the skin to the pink fat below. There were even two faint lines like outer traces where her thumb and little finger had merely grazed the skin. Even as I studied the damage I was wondering how I would explain it to Lillian.

'You deserved it,' Judith said calmly.

'Don't try to justify yourself. You've branded my face

and maybe ruined my life. I was a fool ever to contact you.'

I took my handkerchief from my pocket and attempted to clean the wounds. The mirror began to shake in my hand. All the time I was thinking that, if I had really wanted to, I could have avoided her blows.

'Sit down and I'll do it,' she said. 'You need your ankles seen to as well.'

We looked into each other's eyes. I saw that hers were empty of malice; perhaps I even detected concern. I sat beside her. She made me pull up my trouserlegs, peel down my socks, then sit with my feet up on the bench between us. There seemed to be no end to my indignities.

She told me that the wounds needed antiseptic; I should also consider a tetanus injection. I looked down and saw that the dog's teeth had punctured the skin.

'I keep my injections up to date,' I told her. 'I do too much travelling not to.'

We walked together to a chemist's on the arterial road five hundred yards away. I stood outside pretending nonchalance while Judith went to the till and traffic blundered past.

When she returned she guided me round a corner into a deserted sidestreet with high blank walls. We were like lovers hiding away from the busy world.

I supported myself against a wall while Judith put the finishing touches to her treatment of my face. Even though she smoothed it gently onto my skin the antiseptic stung like the cut of a whip. Despite my resolve I could not prevent tears from coming to my eyes. Embarrassed and ashamed, I wiped them away with the back of my hand.

'Say it was the dog,' she said.

'What?'

'Tell Lillian that you were attacked by a dog. Pretend it was an Alsatian; she'll not know any different.'

'I try not to lie to my wife.'

'Do you want to tell her a small lie or do you want to tell her the whole truth?'

I said nothing. My nostrils smarted with the reek of antiseptic.

'Well then, make it the dog.'

'She'll never believe me. These scratches don't look like claw marks. And the bites were obviously made by a small dog. Besides, Alsatians are too big to attack that low on the body.'

'Then think of a better excuse. And since you mentioned your ankles, I should treat them as well.'

'Leave them. There's no way you can—'

But before I could finish she knelt on the pavement and began to swab the skin on my ankles. Dirt from the pavement was printed on her bare knee.

I did not know whether to look round or not. It was demeaning for us both to be in such a position, like a messiah and his disciple. I did not know what I would do if someone came round the corner to confront us.

'Help me up,' she demanded, raising one hand, 'I've done what I can.'

As I grasped Judith's hand I noticed the lines on her wrists again. My imagination was fired; I saw my daughter struggling helplessly, rope lashed around her limbs, as some appalling ritual took shape.

'I don't understand you,' I said as she stood up.

'I'm not easy enough?'

'You say you respect me and then you rake your nails across my face. You want gifts from me but not money that could be put to better use. You want to meet me and then you want nothing more to do with me.'

'So my attitudes are as contradictory as yours?'

'My attitudes—' I began, and then stopped.

'I'm right. Aren't I?'

'Maybe.'

'Listen to me; there's a truth here that we have to acknowledge. It won't go away if we continue to ignore it.'

'You think not?'

'The truth is we're fascinated by each other.'

I looked at the pavement. A cigarette end lay in the gutter. There was lipstick on the filter. She went on.

'We want to surrender to that fascination and at the same time we want to be free of it. Why? Because we know it's going to be dangerous.'

I said nothing. Traffic hissed past the end of the street.

'We're never going to forget each other, no matter how we try,' Judith insisted. 'If we said goodbye now, and never met again, we would spend what's left of our lives wondering how the other was and what they were doing. We would never be able to rest.'

I shook my head. I didn't want to believe her.

She reached out, took my hand, and squeezed it.

'We have to follow this to the end, Jamie. There's a shape to it that neither of us can quite see. Somehow or other, it has to reach a conclusion.'

4

I should have recognised him as soon as he walked through the doorway.

I had been waiting for Judith for more than fifteen minutes. Although I pretended unconcern, in truth I had read the menu several times and further study would have been perverse. Other tables had steadily filled with those who evidently used the patisserie as a meeting place, and animated conversations were drowning out the Vivaldi tape which I was sure would loop endlessly. Most of the customers were couples, and many were homosexual men. I began to wonder if my solitude would make them think that I was waiting for either an approach or a partner; worse, they could believe that I was as lonely and as friendless as Archie Sproat had been. To add to my unease, a woman at the till kept catching my eye. Each time this happened she smiled as if we were friends, but I did not even know her.

Three times a waitress asked if I was ready to order, and each time I said that I was waiting for someone to join me. At last I decided that I would have a coffee, drink it quickly, and leave. As I began to order a man in his early thirties, wearing a scuffed black denim jacket, came through the doorway. He looked searchingly around the room, saw me, and walked forward.

He had a broad face, a broken nose, and large-pored

skin that would have tanned easily if he had lived a more outdoor life. His black tousled hair was deliberately uncombed and a few specks of dandruff dusted his collar. The waitress stood beside me with her pen almost touching her notepad. I raised a hand to indicate she should wait a moment.

The man looked at me with dark, unfriendly eyes; I sensed contempt in his gaze.

'Mr McGoldrick,' he said with a particular cadence. It was hardly a question.

I nodded. There was only one person he could be. When he spoke again I detected a Mediterranean inflexion; I had not realised that Judith's lover had been born in another country.

'Judith can't be here. She would have telephoned your home if you had given her your number.'

The waitress pursed her lips.

'You're Alex,' I said.

The man nodded curtly.

'She could have rung this number,' I suggested. 'You needn't have come all this way.'

'I volunteered. And she said she wanted to find out a few more things.'

The waitress interrupted us, her voice lightened by exasperation; if Sir did not wish to order, then perhaps . . . I had no desire to create a scene, so I motioned Alex to sit down opposite me and asked if he wanted coffee.

'And something to eat,' he said challengingly and fixed me with a stare. I nodded.

He chose a slice of honey-rich pastry scattered with almonds. We said nothing as it was served with our coffee. As it was laid on the table the crockery clattered like an alarm, sharpening the tension between us.

'You don't mind, do you?' he asked as he picked up a fork and held it above the pastry. I was determined not to respond to insolence, so I said nothing and did not change my expression. He shrugged and began to eat. As he did so I noticed that the index and middle fingers of his right hand were discoloured. Paint emphasised the grain of his skin like a bruise.

I remained motionless until Alex had finished. I did not even drink my coffee. I was acutely aware that the other customers might think that we were lovers.

'I recognised you as soon as I saw you,' he said after a while. A morsel of food clung momentarily to one corner of his mouth before he pushed it onto his lip with his third finger.

'You've seen photographs of me. I'm not too different from them.'

'You're always complacent in them. They're misleading. But in some respects you look like your daughter.'

I leaned forward and kept my voice low. I knew we must resemble conspirators but I was still unwilling to be overheard. 'Why isn't she here? Is this some arrangement between the two of you?'

'Not in the way that you mean it. She's injured.'

'She's hurt?'

'It's nothing serious. A twisted ankle? Sprained? I don't know which is which. I put a bandage around it and told her not to come. We had an argument, but she saw that I was right.'

'If you hadn't volunteered to meet me, would she have come anyway?'

'I'm sure she would.'

There were smears of honey on the surface of the plate. Like a peasant unable to leave any food Alex angled the fork, scraped the honey onto it, and then placed the prongs into his mouth, tightening his lips to draw off all of the sweetness.

'What does she want to know?' I asked.

'I can report that your scratches have healed. I can tell where they were.'

I expected him to lay down the fork but he kept it loosely balanced in one hand, like a weapon, while he picked up his cup with the other.

'She wants to know what you told your wife – Lillian, is it? – about the dog.'

I brooded on the answer I should give.

'Well? Did you tell her?'

'I did, yes.'

'And?' Because I did not answer immediately, he went on. 'Judith wants to know if she believed you.'

'That has nothing to do with either of you. Especially you.'

He put down the fork and leaned a little further forward. I could see the coarse texture of his skin, a small mole on his right cheek, the dull ceramic of a filling in a front tooth.

'She doesn't want to be the cause of a break between you and your wife. If you can set her mind at ease . . .'

'I told Lillian I'd been attacked.'

'By the dog?'

'I said that I'd been leaving the gallery when a strange woman's dog went for my ankles. I said the only way to get it off me was to kick it. I said I'd never seen the owner before, but that she went insane. She raked her nails down my cheek and then walked away with the animal as if nothing had happened.'

'That was ingenious. She believed you?'

'Of course.'

He stared at me. I looked down. I was not certain that Lillian had been fully convinced. She had let the matter drop, but not before telling me that I should have reported the incident to the police, who should have charged the woman with actual bodily harm. I'd been too shocked to do anything, I responded; anyway, it wouldn't have been worth it, for the poor woman was obviously off her head.

'I'll tell Judith you talked your way out of it,' Alex said.

My resentment sharpened into anger. 'You can tell her that I'm surprised I didn't lay her out cold. Years ago I might have done that.'

'I understand. Did you do that with her mother?'

I made no reply, for I was scared to give myself away. Two or three times, no more, my frustration had become so charged, so overpowering, that I had taken it out on Eve. I had never hit anyone since.

'Perhaps she deserved it,' Alex said. Although he struggled to keep his sentence free of emphasis, a smoky relish broke through.

I did not know which woman he meant.

He gave an unexpectedly pleasant smile. 'I am sorry to be so direct. Judith and I have no talent for—' He paused to select his next word.

'Diplomacy,' I suggested. 'Consideration.'

'Circumlocution.' He produced the word proudly, as if he had just learned it.

'If that's true then you'll have no difficulty in telling me what your relationship is. You'll be able to tell me exactly and without—' And here, too, I allowed myself an identical pause, 'Circumlocution.'

'You suspect me,' he said.

'We suspect each other. Don't we?'

He considered this for a moment, and then asked was I not going to drink my coffee. I said I was not thirsty. He took my cup from me and drank it himself.

Despite myself I looked down the room towards the cashier. She was counting out change for a customer. In the few seconds that it took to study her I saw that her hair was dyed ash-blonde and that she was probably the same age as me, although the years had not been kind to her. I was certain that I had never met her before. Then she looked up and gave me another smile, but more cautiously this time. It was slightly uneven, as if part of her mouth had been frozen.

She recognises me, I thought; she's seen my photograph somewhere. Maybe she even likes modern sculpture.

I dropped my gaze to Alex's hands. They looked as if they had been smeared by fingerprint ink.

'What do you think of Judith?' he asked.

I would not be diverted. 'Aren't you going to answer me?'

'Judith told me you had no interest in her life. Why the change to responsible parent? It's far too late for that.'

'You don't want to answer. There's something you want to keep secret.'

'You're not in a position to lecture others on secrets,' he said. His features were darker now; he was no stranger to cruelty, I began to realise. And I decided that his was an archetypal face, one that had been common to thousands. Stoics, orators, adventurers, murderers had borne the same impassive darkness.

'You're much more nervous than I expected,' Alex went on. 'There's no need to be.'

I found I was tapping my fingers on the table like an impatient interrogator, and had no idea how long I had been doing so. I stopped immediately and raised one hand to my face, letting the fingers rest on my injured cheek.

Alex took the movement as a cue. 'Well-balanced, do you think?' Although he mentioned no name, I still understood who he meant.

'I thought she was until she did this.'

'Sometimes violence becomes necessary. Sometimes we are not allowed any other means of expression.'

'I'm still waiting for your answer. About trust.'

He put down the empty cup of coffee and slid it across the table so that once again it rested in front of me.

'You are worried about my hold over her. Don't be. Judith is a free woman. She owes me nothing. Whenever she wants to, she can walk away.'

'You sound like a master, forever promising freedom to his slave.'

He could not suppress a smirk. He was taking pleasure in his own intelligence, and for a few seconds his eyes shone like bright liquid. I realised that he had anticipated my questions.

He leaned forward in an invitation. I wanted to edge away, but I forced myself to mirror him. A change in the light emphasised the old fracture of his nose.

'We are lovers,' he murmured. I could smell honey and caffeine on his breath. 'We confide in each other. We each know the other's reactions. We are familiar with every square centimetre of the other's body.'

He spoke with the artful passion of a man claiming ownership. Even though I tried to force them away, images of my daughter and this man condensed in the cloudy turbulence of my imagination like spirits summoned by a medium.

Alex held the pause before he spoke again, his voice a whisper of temptation.

'Perhaps you are excited by this? Your daughter is a very attractive woman.'

All I could do was shake my head unconvincingly.

Still he waited before he spoke again. 'But I told you there was no need to worry. Judith is safe now. She has a haven, a home, a friend. I rescued her.'

'What do you mean – rescued?'

He waved a hand between us as if he were brushing away an imaginary fly. Suddenly I was suspicious and nervous of our surroundings.

'Look,' I said, 'can we get out of here?'

'Judith said that, at the zoo, you were in a panic to leave the bird house, as well.'

'For the same reasons. If we must have this conversation, I'd rather have it where we couldn't be overheard. Are we going or not?'

'No one can hear us. Look at them. They are too wrapped up in themselves.' He raised his hands palm upwards to indicate the other customers, then put them flat on the table. 'Besides, I'm comfortable. And I'm still thirsty.'

I ordered another coffee. When she served it the waitress tore the bill from her pad and left it beside me. I asked Alex who or what he had rescued Judith from.

'The kind of life she was living. She had an unhappy time with the Fords. They were bigots who thought she should treat them like saints. They believed she owed her life to them, and that she should spend it giving them thanks. I was the first person to rescue her and ask nothing.'

'Rescue her from what? Drugs? Other people?'

He shrugged. 'A little of both. There was a man who was no good. He wasn't important; she soon realised how little she really thought of him. Which of us hasn't made mistakes over other people? And she was not an addict. Her drugs were . . . recreational. But we're clean now. Both of us. I give you my word.'

'When you met, you weren't clean either?'

'I smoked a little dope. You cannot disapprove of such an ordinary vice. And when I persuaded Judith to stop, I stopped too.' He raised a hand again, this time to gesture at the side of his head. 'You have to be sane and level-headed to do even the softer drugs. If not, they twist any sickness deeper into the mind.'

'My daughter is mentally unstable – is that what you're telling me?'

'I wouldn't put it so harshly. She has moments of—' And he stopped.

At that moment I suddenly knew the word he was on the brink of saying. I spoke it for him.

'Depression,' I said.

He nodded. 'You told her that her mother suffered, too.'

It was true. Judith had known more than I had realised; she had even begun to sketch the symptoms for me.

'I wished I hadn't,' I confessed.

'But you did. And now the harm has been done. She believes she may have inherited the illness.'

'There's no evidence that depression is inherited,' I answered with as much conviction as I could muster, although I did not know if what I claimed was true.

'But that's what she fears. Judith is very sensitive. She tells me what she sometimes feels. She says it's like being at the edge of a whirlpool. Each minute carries her closer to the centre, each minute brings her nearer to being dragged under. Hope exhausts itself because there is no alternative to catastrophe. No doubt her mother felt the same.'

'She wouldn't do what her mother did.'

'You think not?'

'Eve was an extreme case.'

'Perhaps. I take it you've noticed Judith's wrists?'

His eyes were bright and emotionless as a bird's. I could no longer meet his gaze, and looked down. My left leg was trembling. I was pressing my foot hard on the floor like a driver braking before a crash, and until I noticed the tremor I did not even realise that I was doing it.

'You needn't worry,' he went on. 'Those are old marks, years old. They were made before I met her.'

This time I forced myself to look him in the face. 'Why would she want to cut her wrists?'

'You lived with her mother. You can answer that better than I can.'

'And you claim to have rescued her.'

He nodded. 'I wanted a model. I was studying Schiele, and thought his compositions could be used as starting points for my own work, like Velasquez's were used by Picasso. I didn't know where this would lead; it may have been to total failure. But a friend teaching at a college told me he knew an amateur model with a Schiele look about her. I made contact. It was Judith.'

'She doesn't look like—'

'She did in those days. She spent little on food, less on herself. Her face had an authentic, haunted, tubercular look. Schiele would have loved her.'

'The work?'

'Some was good enough to keep. Would you like to see it?'

'You must be crazy. Schiele's real talent was for courting outrage. His was a superficial and exploitative art. It worries and offends me that you used Judith in such a way. You were putting her in as much danger as anyone else ever did.'

'You detest one of the greats? Perhaps I shouldn't be surprised. Someone like yourself would find Mondrian more humane, and he painted like a mere mathematician. But you're wrong on many things. I was determined not to exploit Judith. And I did not.'

'No? You painted her as a Schiele nude?'

He gave a small exhalation of breath that carried a faint derisory whistle within it. 'She modelled naked at the college, but not for me. I saw that she was too fragile for that.'

'Was that the start of your relationship?'

'We weren't lovers.'

'When did that happen?'

'A while later. Months.'

'She left another boyfriend for you?'

'Yes. He wasn't a good man. He didn't care about her.'

'You do?'

'Isn't that obvious?'

There was a crash of crockery from behind the counter that made several customers look towards it. We did not take our eyes off each other. Out of the corner of mine I could just see the blonde cashier looking over at the source of the accident.

'There was an instinct in Judith,' he went on. 'She knew it was better to keep a distance between the man and herself. She lived on her own, although where she lived was filthy and cold. It was a squat. There was no water, no electricity, no heat. The front door was boarded up. To get into the house she climbed on top of a brick wall and then lifted a sash window from the outside.'

'Usually people share squats. They did when I was a student. I was even in one myself for a while.'

'There were others but they had all moved out. Only Judith was left. She slept on the floor in an old eiderdown that was sewn together to make a sleeping-bag. There were a few candles, some tins of food, a heater that campers use. The other rooms were full of debris – empty cans and crisp packets, a mattress with its springs sticking out, bits of clothing.'

'They hadn't left their clothes.'

'I said *bits*. A shirt that had been ripped into pieces, the back pocket from a pair of jeans, torn stockings – that kind of thing. There was mouse shit all over the floor. I was disturbed that mice ran over pieces of clothing and tugged them around. In my country we never treat clothes in such an offhand way. I picked them off the floor and hung them out of reach on shelves and windowsills and mantelpieces. I even tied some onto light fittings. By the time I left, the place looked like the catacombs we have at home, where people fasten offerings to trees and leave pieces of clothing wedged between stones.'

Apparently thinking his own behaviour rather strange, Alex lapsed into silence.

'You moved her out,' I prompted.

'As soon as I could, without telling the boyfriend. It was a humane act, not a selfish one. I didn't want Judith to live in my house. She would get in the way of my work and my other friendships. I told her she could stay while she sorted out her life. I thought it would take a few weeks, maybe two months at the most. But that was—' And he stopped while he thought about the length of time. 'Almost three years ago.'

'It just happened,' I said, unable to keep the salt of irony from my voice.

He answered immediately, and I understood that he was responding to what he saw as a challenge. 'That's right. Neither of us suspected it would happen.'

'Come on,' I said. 'You can't tell me that you invited a young woman into your house and that—'

'That,' he insisted, 'is what I'm telling you. If you were a normal father you would thank me for saving your daughter.'

He paused, daring me to contradict him.

'Yes,' I said, 'I believe you did. But I would guess that neither of you think your arrangement is permanent.'

'And if it is not, why should you be interested?'

I hesitated. 'The same reason I've become interested in her welfare.'

Again he smiled, and again it carried a metallic tang of self-congratulation.

'You can't cut yourself free, can you?' he asked.

'No. Can you?'

His smile vanished as suddenly as if his face had been

slapped, and in its place was a puzzled, slightly perplexed look.

'I'm her father. I don't like it and I've even tried to forget it. I know that compared to other fathers I have complicated emotions, even distant ones. But I can't forget her. Not just yet.'

'Conscience?'

'Call it what you want. I've come to a decision, Mr – I don't know your last name.'

'Stylianou.'

Over the past twenty years I had become adept at pronouncing unusual names; Alex's was easy, yet I did not want to repeat it in case I stumbled over it.

'My decision is to help Judith. I don't mean that I'll always be there; I won't be. But for the moment she needs two things from me.'

He held up one finger. I responded as if to a conditioned reflex.

'She needs to know who I am,' I explained. 'It doesn't matter if she doesn't like me. And it doesn't matter if what she thinks about me is limited or misleading or just plain wrong. There's some mechanism inside her that wants to give an identity to her father. I should help. No one else can.'

'You say her opinion of you may be limited. It *has* to be limited. Officially you don't acknowledge her existence. She only has partial access to you, and that is always on your terms.'

Now Alex held up a second finger. I breathed deeply to suppress my irritation.

'And she needs some kind of security. I don't mean emotional security; I can't give her that. But I can maybe help in other ways.'

'She told me she tore up your cheque.'

'And did she tell you she asked me to buy paint for you?'

He shook his head. There was a burst of laughter from one of the tables behind. I knew that it did not concern us, but I nevertheless lowered my voice as if we had been overheard.

'I refused,' I told Alex. 'My help is for her, not for you. We all have to be very clear about that.'

'I have a keener sense of duty than you ever had. I cannot take charity, even though it would only have been a fraction of your money.'

I used his Christian name for the first time. 'Alex, you'd be a fool if you didn't. But I'm not going to offer it to you. My concern is for Judith; that's all.'

'We're not separate people. You can't help one of us without helping the other. We are closer than you seem able to grasp. We have more in common than you believe possible.'

'I don't think so.'

'No? Shall I tell you what happens when someone is rescued from danger? They spend the rest of their lives thinking what would have happened if they hadn't been snatched from the edge. They realise that they are who they are only because of the person who rescued them.'

'That's a flawed basis for a long-term relationship.'

A look of disdain came over his face. 'What do you know of salvation?'

'Probably a lot more than you.'

He looked down at his hands. His right thumb was pushed so hard into the middle of his left palm that the fingers had curled around it in a half-closed fist.

'Have you ever been saved from danger?'

'No,' I answered, but wondered if I should have said yes.

'I'm a Cypriot; you know that?'

'So?'

'When I was a young boy I was taken from my village.

Why? Because we would have been murdered if we had stayed there. We fled south across the mountains. The Turks were so close behind us we feared that each hour could be our last. Some of my relatives were killed, and many of my neighbours. We were hounded from homes our families had owned for generations.'

I said nothing. I knew little of the invasion other than that it had been in the wake of sectarian butchery, and that the war itself had been characterised by racism and brutality on both sides. Perhaps for as long as Alex could remember his life had been filled with rumours, with tales of vendetta and reprisal. I was sure that, if I asked him, he would recite for me a chronicle of offence, a litany of the dead.

'I can never go back there,' he said with the quiet passion of a refugee. 'Not until the Attila line is down. My birthplace is denied to me until my country is whole again. I have that in common with your daughter, too. We are like trees whose taproots have been severed. She has regained a lost part of her past. I know that mine can never be recovered.'

For a short while he brooded, his mind elsewhere. I decided that talk of childhood would always lead him into such reveries.

I had no such nostalgia for my own birthplace. Instead it seemed to me to have been nothing more than an unfortunate accident that I was born where I had been.

My parents had fled from a succession of failures, until at last they found a home in an old farm set on high, bleak moors. Cold inhabited the stonework. Constant gales cuffed the chimneys and sent smoke billowing out of the fireplaces so that the rooms always had the acrid, suffocating smell of burning.

I couldn't wait to escape to the city, lose my accent, forget my past. I read whatever I could find, and spent much of my time in a kind of dream, imagining histories and cities fit only for the heroic. Everything in the outside world was strange, inviting, unknown, and my secret fear was that it would remain unknowable.

Only later did I come to believe that my desire to alter landscapes, to charge them with meaning, had had its beginnings among those endless miles of turf and rush and heather. And although I had never acknowledged it, many of my early works had sprung directly from the other world that had lain at the very edge of my childhood. Only when it was nearing completion did I recognise that my shining equatorial needle was similar to an exhibit at the Festival of Britain, which I had read about but been unable to visit; the ridge of bronze panels shown on my book jacket was a secret nod to comic-book pictures of a stegosaurus that had lumbered through my infant dreams; my Interlocking Pieces had inherited qualities of assembly and shape from a puzzle my father had once bought me.

Alex, suddenly as alert as any hunter, looked up at me with wide, unblinking eyes. 'Come to see her,' he said.

Before I could refuse he spoke again, this time more excitedly.

'Come to see her now. You'll understand each other better if you do.'

'I'll ring her sometime. I promise.'

'You've somewhere else to go?'

I hesitated for a moment. If I had invented another appointment then that single miss of a beat would have been enough to signal my lie.

'When you last spoke to Judith you said your wife was away. Is that still true?'

Before I could reply he reached across the table and took hold of my wrist. I lifted my arm away, twisting it from his grip, but this did not deter him.

'We'll not ring her. She'll be expecting me but not you. We'll surprise her. Judith would like you to see how we live. It may remind you of the days before your success – and it will give you a clearer idea of how you can help her. But we should leave now. It's twenty minutes by train.'

'I don't know,' I said, picking up the bill. As I did so I looked again at the woman at the cash desk. This time she averted her eyes.

'You've nothing to lose,' Alex said. It was almost an accusation.

No, I thought, I don't; I had already lost my peace of mind.

'All right,' I said, and as I got to my feet he bunched his fists together like a triumphant sportsman.

I walked to the till and opened my wallet. The cashier looked at me with her awkward, lopsided smile. There was loose skin on her neck and deep lines around her mouth and eyes.

'You don't remember me, do you?' she asked.

Conscious all the time of Alex standing behind me, I looked steadily at her. Now that we were close I recognised a suggestion of resemblance, even of lost familiarity. Her hair was evidently dyed, as the roots were grey, and her face had a harried, stiffened look, as if she had suffered misfortune upon misfortune.

'I've changed,' she mumbled as she took the payment from me. It was like an apology. She searched so energetically for the change that the coins clattered in their moulded trays. 'I've had several strokes, you see, and it's altered my face. I shouldn't have expected you to realise; the doctors all say I'm far too young to have had them. How are you, anyway? Are you well?'

'I'm fine,' I said, perplexed.

As she put the change into my hand the woman's fingers lingered for a moment with the nails touching my palm. Our eyes met again. Suddenly I knew that I knew her, and my heart lurched.

'I often think of you, Mick,' she said. 'It's Angie. Do you remember me now?'

I clutched the coins tightly, like a man hanging onto a bribe. Alex shuffled behind me.

'I expected you that next week, but you never came,' she went on. 'Still, it's all a long time in the past now. But I've often wondered if you carried on with your art work. Did you?'

'I think you've got the wrong person,' I said. I wanted to step away but could not.

Angie looked at me carefully. I was shamed by her gaze.

'I can't have,' she insisted.

'My name's not Mick. And I'm not an artist.'

After a pause she said 'I'm sorry,' but she plainly did not believe me. 'I understand,' she added quietly, like someone humiliated.

I broke away and stepped towards the door. Alex opened it for us.

'Whoever this Mick is, I hope you meet him sometime,' I said, desperately maintaining the pretence.

She shook her blonded head. 'No,' she said, 'I don't think I want to meet him any more.'

It was a relief to be outside, but I turned to Alex with assumed exasperation. 'Stupid woman,' I said, 'what can you do if they insist you're someone else?'

'Nothing,' he answered. In the daylight he looked pale and feral. I dared not let the meeting with Angie rest.

'Obviously she was confusing me with another artist. It seemed simpler to deny that I am one. Otherwise things would have got even more complicated.'

'You could have told her you were a sculptor. What harm would it have done?'

'If you're successful you learn to avoid scenes like that. Some people think they're your friend, even if you've never met them. Maybe you learned a lesson from it, Alex.'

'I understand.'

'Good,' I said.

We were several steps away from the entrance by now. Already I had determined never to go back there. And it would be prudent, I thought, never even to pass by its doors.

There were problems on the line. Before it crawled into each station the train stopped for minutes on end, so our rackety, swaying journey was punctuated by awkward periods of stasis. At such times I looked out of the window onto banking thick with weeds, or rat-grey walls with ducting snaked along them. But soon my attention was drawn further up the carriage.

Three people sat together: a middle-aged man and woman and an overplump girl who must have been their daughter. The girl was aged about thirteen, but she was dressed like someone much younger, in a thin blue dress with tiny white spots and an unbuttoned pink cardigan – a child's outfit. Her father was a thin, unobtrusive man with a trim moustache who whispered into her ear, and as she listened her eyes shone with something between laughter and tears. Every few minutes his hands swooped on the girl, grabbed her, probed, tickled. He caught her under her arms and chin, above her hip and on her legs. Her squeals were somewhere between terror and glee. She tried to beat him off but his bony fingers could always move faster than her pudgy hands. As she jumped and twisted, her child's skirt rode up high on large, pale thighs which seemed to have the consistency of dough. All the time the girl's mother read a magazine with a tight, inflexible smile on her face. Sometimes her head gave a rolling motion that could have meant either distance or assent.

The other passengers read their newspapers or stared unseeingly out of the windows as if nothing unusual was happening. I was fascinated and repelled, and also found myself trying to avoid looking at the family. Alex, however, stared unblinkingly at them for the entire journey.

'For God's sake,' I muttered, 'they can see you watching.'

'I know,' he said, but did not avert his eyes.

As we drew into our station the man put both hands into his daughter's armpits and spread his thumbs near the top of her breasts. She screeched hysterically.

'Alex,' I said, 'aren't we here?'

An observer disturbed at his task, Alex looked at me with an unexpected distance in his eyes. 'Yes,' he said, and stood up. Once on his feet he swayed a little, even though the train had stopped, and when we walked down the platform he was still looking at the family through the dusty windows.

The station's exit booth was unmanned. We walked out onto a busy crossroad with its other corners crowded by a petrol station, a tiny grocer's that called itself a supermarket, and a pub whose walls curved outwards like a fortification.

'I don't think I've been here before,' I said, but Alex was already leading the way towards a pedestrian crossing.

We walked down an arterial road past a newsagent's and a video store, and after a few minutes turned the corner into a street of terraced houses set back from the pavement behind tiny gardens. None of them was well-kept and some were strewn with crushed cans and old pieces of carpet. I counted the numbers as we walked. For reasons which could not have been rational, I was worried that Alex's house would be the one with the battered skeletal pram outside the front door. When I realised that it could not be, and that we were five numb-ers further on, I breathed out with relief that made my chest feel light. I had been holding air in my lungs for several yards.

Alex pressed the bell before he put his key in the lock, and I knew he was signalling to Judith before we entered.

A bicycle stood on the cracked and scaled linoleum in the hallway. We edged past it into the front room, where Judith sat watching television. She wore a white T-shirt and fawn leggings, and had both legs crooked over the arm of the chair. One of her ankles was tightly bandaged. She did not attempt to get up and did not even smile.

'I didn't expect two of you,' she told Alex. I did not know if I should believe her. Television sound furred the air around us.

'A father should see how his daughter lives,' Alex said.

Instinctively I looked for my book. A few volumes had been arranged on a shelf in an alcove beside the chimney-breast. Above them, incongruously, a black-and-white print of a photograph from the Cyprus emergency hung on the wall. A man lay sprawled on the floor of a house, one arm thrown back, his eyes as bright and dead as sunlit ice, a pool of thickened blood on the flagstones beneath his head. A family of witnesses, old women and a young boy, stared at the camera, mute with the enormity of their loss, too stunned to know what to do next. I had seen this image countless times; it had become emblematic of the island's agony. It was an instant in time whose very familiarity was unsettling. It seemed unnecessary and exploitative for Alex to have such anguish so prominently on display.

Beneath the print, beside a heap of dog-eared art magazines weighed down by a piece of pottery, was my book. I had had a secret fear that it might have been torn and despoiled, but it appeared to have been treated with a collector's care. Beside it, and in far worse condition, were volumes on art history and individual painters, including two on Goya. There was also a *Psychology For Beginners* and several books on the history and culture of Cyprus.

'Sorry about the ankle,' I said to Judith.

'My own stupid fault.'

'Does it hurt?'

She grimaced.

The suspicion grew within me that there was little wrong with her, and that I had walked unthinkingly into a simple but effective trap.

Alex prompted her. 'You complained of a headache as well.'

Judith put her fingers to her temples and flicked them outwards to indicate dispersal.

'Can't you turn that off?' he asked, and before she could reply he leaned over and pressed the television control button. The picture collapsed in on itself and took the noise with it.

'He wanted to come here,' Alex explained.

It was a distortion but I did not protest.

Judith spread her arms in parody. 'Should I point out its features like a good estate agent?'

'That's not funny,' Alex said.

'No? Aren't you laughing at us, Jamie? Don't you think our poverty is ever-so-slightly amusing? You shouldn't have brought him, Alex.'

'You said you wanted him to visit us.'

'And now that he's here I can see that I was wrong.'

'You spent your first few months in worse conditions than this,' I told her.

Alex showed me into a small dining room and kitchen while Judith hobbled behind us, supporting her weight by leaning on the door jamb. Posters from exhibitions had been tacked to the walls. In the middle of the room was a circular table that looked as if it had been stolen from a bar. There were also several chairs and stools. None of them matched.

'So now you know how we live,' Judith said. She was like a plaintiff who had just seen her evidence displayed.

'The bedrooms and bathroom are upstairs,' Alex added.

'And where do you work?'

'In the big bedroom,' Judith said. 'He uses that one because there's more light. Do you want to see it?'

'I can't help. I've already told you.'

'You should still see it. Come with me.'

'Judith,' Alex said warningly, 'your father has doubts about my talent.'

'Have you seen any of Alex's work?' she asked.

'No.'

'Then you can have doubts after you've seen it, not before.'

On the stairs Judith became more mobile, ascending them energetically and apparently without hindrance. Once at the top, however, she raised her bandaged foot from the ground and massaged it with one hand.

The bedroom they slept in was cramped and gloomy, with curtains that were still closed. I imagined that a smell of nakedness and sex still clung to the tangled bedclothes like a warm mist, and was pleased when Judith made a point of closing the door.

'This room,' she said.

The room smelled of turpentine and linseed. There was a desk with a wooden stool, a standing easel and a closed one leaning against the windowsill, tubes and boxes of paint, jars of brushes, boxes of pencils and pens, and hundreds of sketches and paintings. Some had been rolled up and stacked in corners, others had been nailed onto home-made frames and were leaning one on top of the other, and several drawings had been tacked to the walls. Every one was representational, the majority were figurative, and most of those were portaits of either fellow Cypriots, or Judith, or of Alex himself.

'So?' she asked.

'He has energy; I'll grant you that.'

'I think the word is talent. It may even be genius.'

'I might accept talent, nothing more.'

'He can see people and sketch them straight away – can't you, Alex? He could sit down now and draw the people who sat opposite you on the train.'

'A bit like a pavement artist,' I murmured as I studied the portraits.

Most, I had to admit, were quite successful. They had been executed with an economy of touch, and demonstrated both sympathy and detailed observation. Some, however, were forced, laborious, their sitters coarsened with over-heavy features. Perhaps Alex's talent was unpredictable; perhaps it favoured him at times only to desert him later. Most unsettling of all was the inconstancy of the style. All of his work was derivative, but like an unsure student he had plundered the techniques and themes of one artist after another, seemingly finding each one wanting. Here was Judith in the manner of Schiele, of Modigliani, of Blue Period Picasso; here was a dark-haired Mediterranean in an open-necked shirt, his face seen through the same styles. The man was handsome in a peasant sort of way, with a moustache that gave him a charmless resemblance to a brigand, but in many of the studies his face appeared set and inflexible.

'How many has he done of you?' I asked Judith.

'Thousands.'

'Hundreds,' Alex corrected her.

'And you haven't finished yet?'

'Of course not. I don't expect to ever stop working on my subjects. You wouldn't ask such questions of Bonnard or Wyeth. But you probably don't admire their work either.' It was not a question.

'Put it this way,' I said; 'it's impossible to be innovative in figurative work now. The age has ended. You just have to look at contemporary portraits to see that decadence has set in.'

'You don't think I'm good. You don't think I *can* be good.'

'It's not that. Of course you can be good. You can't be at the vanguard, that's all. Nowadays the only real progress is made by artists who are less concerned with the apparent look of things, who've stopped being interested in mere surface.'

'Like you, you mean,' Judith said.

I ignored her. 'Perhaps your real talent is as an illustrator,' I suggested to Alex.

'There's no shame in illustration. But I don't want to be a mere illustrator. My ambition is greater than that.'

'A lot of us have to settle for less than our ambition.'

'Did you?'

I conceded his point. 'But you're going to have to make changes. To begin with, you're obsessed by certain subjects. Only a genius could be so productive from such a narrow range.'

'It's true. Some images I have to return to time and time again.'

'Exactly.'

'Not because I want to, but because I have no choice. Why do you smile?'

'I'm sorry.'

'No, tell me why.'

'Because you have a highly romantic notion of art. You have no choice, you say – but in fact you do.'

He raised his hands in a gesture of refusal.

'Believe me,' I insisted, 'it's only when artists become critically selective that they progress. Those stories about the tormented genius, the artist who is a channel for some kind of mysterious natural force of creation – they're good for the press, that's all. Only innocent dupes who idolise Van Gogh believe in that kind of myth. True art, *real* art is calculated, even clinical. Those masterpieces the public thinks of as immediate and passionate and unrestrained are carefully judged, all of them. They're balanced, reflexive, symbolic, geometrical. They had to be. You can't sustain passion over months.'

'So your advice to me?'

'Don't be spendthrift with your talent; you're spreading it across several styles and it's getting thin. Look – can't you see how some pieces are much more lively and effective than others? If you want to improve them, allow yourself a little cynicism. Forget about your original motivation and think in terms of technique.'

'But I have to portray Judith. I can't ignore her. She's a subject I can never exhaust.'

'I see. And your own face?'

'The same.'

'And the man with a moustache? I'll take him as an example. Is he inexhaustible as well?'

'My father.'

'Right. Well, there's a remarkable variation in quality in the way you've pictured him. Look, here – the musculature of the face has seized. It's bad technique. The man looks incapable of movement. I know he's your father, but you must forget what's important to you; you'll be a better artist.'

'You fool, Jamie,' Judith said.

'I know what I'm talking about,' I said sharply.

'Fool,' she repeated.

'I don't think you recognise him,' Alex said. 'The photograph downstairs.'

I caught my breath for a moment. 'That's him?'

No one answered. And now I realised, too, who the boy

was who had been caught by the photographer as he stood in the death room with his family.

'I'm sorry,' I said weakly.

I thought of Alex producing image after image of the dead face, as if its reproduction would help him come to terms with the randomness and savagery of his father's killing.

'Why else do you think I have that photograph on my wall?' he asked bitterly.

'It was thoughtless of me. I'm sorry.'

'He was murdered by people he had known for years. Soon after that the Turks invaded. Now I can't even visit his grave.'

I looked down at the floorboards.

'I owe him everything. And I can never repay him. A man can never repay the dead.'

I did not contradict him. He went on.

'And how can you condemn me for my work?'

'I didn't.'

'*I* don't choose these subjects; they choose *me*. I live here in these conditions because it's the price I have to pay. I've taken jobs that almost ruined me because I needed money for materials. I've gone hungry because I spent money on paint rather than on food. And yet I can't sell work which I know is important, which speaks of things that no one else can say. Why? Because dealers and buyers no longer want the truth. They are no longer interested in insight or humanity. What do they want instead? Abstracts. *Abstracts*. Rothko. David Smith. Christo. Paintings with one colour saturating them. Canvas after canvas, the same thick unvaried colour. Ugly chunks of metal welded together like a failed piece of engineering. Sheets of plastic draped and wrapped around statues, cliffs, whole islands. And now we have machines. Grey robots that do nothing but shake pools of mercury and spray black paint on white walls.'

I was the next to be accused; I was sure of it. But the challenge did not come.

'I know it's difficult,' I said.

'The age of abstraction is dying. Its days are numbered. A good critic would read the symptoms like a physician. It's time for tradition to assert itself in a new form.' He stopped for a moment to consider his own prophecy, and when he spoke again there was a touch of despair in his voice. 'How long did you live like this?' he asked.

'Not long. A couple of years. Success came early.'

'Then you cannot know how difficult it is. You can only imagine.'

'I'm not an enemy, Alex,' I said, and regretted the words as soon as I had spoken them. I did not even think that they were true.

'Alex is right,' Judith said. 'There are successful artists earning lots of money who don't have a fraction of his talent. It's difficult to sustain a belief in yourself when the art market is like it is.'

'It's not always the best who rise to the top,' I agreed. Again I had left myself open; again I waited for an accusation. None came.

'You're comfortable now,' Judith continued. 'You don't have to worry about the rent or paying the electricity bill. Your only problem must be grading your commissions in terms of importance and income and the amount of time they take.'

'You can't have any idea how hard I work.'

'I think you may have forgotten what hard work is.'

'Judith, I need no lessons from someone who has been incapable of holding down even the simplest of jobs.'

'And I need none from a man who was incapable of feeling anything for his only child.'

I felt coldness settle on my face like a thin mask, numbing the muscles, making the blood retract.

'Was that unfair?' she asked after a pause.

'It was unfeeling.'

'But not unfair?'

'I think I should leave now.'

'I don't want you to.'

'Stay with us,' Alex said. His voice had quietened, but it was still vaguely threatening. 'You weren't to know what happened to my father. It's my failure that these portraits don't make it clear.'

'This relationship can't work,' I said. 'I was a fool to let myself be carried along this far. We should end it now.'

'We can't end it until it's run its course,' Judith insisted.

'Don't you think it has done?'

'There are still things I need to know.'

'There's nothing else. There's no big secret, Judith. I've told you all there is.'

She put a hand to my face and let the fingers rest lightly on my cheek where she had marked it.

'I want to know how you live,' she said.

'You know what I do. Only a minute ago you were claiming I had no problems.'

'And you were claiming that you had. I want to see where you work, Jamie. When I think of you dreaming up your projects, making plans and models of them, I want to be able to hold an image in my mind.'

I pulled away from her fingers. Her hand stayed frozen in mid-air, then advanced slightly and touched me again. As it did, her sleeve slid a little down her arm and I saw a thin white mark running across the underside of her wrist.

'That would be difficult,' I said.

She shook her head. 'Easy,' she murmured. '*Easy*. It's only a taxi-ride away.'

There were four messages on the answerphone. Because Judith and Alex were within earshot I hesitated before playing them back, but I also worried in case some might be exceptionally urgent. None was. Ken Takama's secretary confirmed a lunch appointment for three days' time; my American agent was optimistic about a possible commission from a Californian foundation; Terry Evans had rung to say that he had a photocopy of an article about the Peermain estate that I might like to have.

And Lillian was sorry, but she would not be home by noon tomorrow; it now looked as if it would be late afternoon by the time she arrived. She added, as she always did, that she loved me.

Judith and Alex pretended not to listen, but I knew that they were taking in each word. I was also certain that Alex had seen and memorised my telephone number.

I showed them round the house with the caution of a man unable to trust his guests. At first they stood quietly with folded arms or walked with their hands in their pockets. Soon they grew more confident, and reached out inquisitively to touch whatever took their interest – furniture, awards, CDs, books, wall hangings from Morocco, an aboriginal painting from Australia, a neon-and-perspex sculpture from New York. Sometimes they asked questions about monetary value which I could not or would not answer.

Judith was fascinated by the wall of photographs in the study. 'This is like a hunter's trophy room,' she said.

My own face, ageing over more than twenty years, stared out of every one of these formal, unvarying records. Sometimes Lillian or Claire stood beside me as I shook a benefactor's hand, a recipient's stiff smile on my lips. My other hand always held the corner of an envelope or a moulded award.

'Your wife doesn't always go with you,' Judith said.

'We travel together whenever we can. She has her own career.'

'I don't see it here.'

'It doesn't rely on patronage or commissions.'

'I see. I suppose she's quite good-looking for someone her age. Is she better looking than my mother?'

I did not want to answer and Judith did not expect one. Instead she pointed to another of the photographs. Claire stood beside Lillian and myself; the award had been given in Paris.

'Your adopted daughter?'

'Yes, that's Claire; taken when she was eighteen. That was three years ago. She came with us whenever we could take her.'

'Has she left home for good?'

'She's taking a business degree in America. She'll be a good businesswoman. She takes after her mother.'

'Her mother?'

'Lillian. You know I mean Lillian.'

'And those are her postcards pinned up on your year planner, I suppose. How different is she to me?'

I had to be careful what I said. 'She moves in different circles.'

'She's more confident than me, is she? More disciplined? Socially adept, with a wide range of influential friends?'

I shrugged.

'You needn't be wary of agreeing, Jamie. I know that what I say must be true. You gave her all the advantages. You gave nothing to me.'

'If you'd like to see my workroom,' I said icily, 'it's at the top of the house. But you mustn't disturb anything.'

'You needn't warn us,' Alex said in a voice of mild reproof.

On the way upstairs Judith asked where we slept. I told her we had four bedrooms; Claire's was kept as she wanted it and the other two were kept for guests. She asked who visited us. I mentioned names that meant nothing to her, but which were familiar to Alex. He gave a wry smile as a signal that he understood the breadth of my acquaintance.

'But you're alone tonight,' Judith said, bending to massage her ankle.

'You can't sleep here.'

She did not straighten up, but raised her head to look directly at me. 'Are we so unlikeable?'

I glanced at Alex. His face was expressionless above his folded arms.

'You know the reasons,' I told them.

'No,' she answered, and straightened up. Her injured foot was bent so that the toe of her shoe pressed into the floor like a ballerina's.

'It's enough that I've let you in here. What would Lillian say if she found out? I could never explain you away.'

'We're fellow-artists and admirers of your work,' Alex suggested. 'You're considering employing us as assistants on your new project.'

'Lillian's not going to find out,' Judith said. She used my wife's name with a slithery familiarity. 'She's not even back here until late tomorrow.'

'You pretended not to listen to those messages,' I said.

Judith began to move forward and then lost her balance so that she had to reach out and steady herself against my arm. I wondered if this were a carefully planned and executed move.

'It would be the first time for almost twenty-five years that we could sleep under the same roof together,' she said.

I took her hands in mine so that she could regain her equilibrium. Instead I felt the increase in pressure as she angled her body forward. She would have fallen to the ground if I had not supported her.

'This door is locked,' I explained. 'You'll have to stand on your own.'

She moved apart from me while I reached for the keys in my pocket.

In the studio it was only a few seconds before confidence, or perhaps this time bravado, animated Judith and Alex. They touched the corner of my desk, the mantelpiece stocked with mementoes of my travels, my chair, the upper edge of a locked filing cabinet.

'What are these?' Alex asked, seeing Ken Takama's photographs on top of the desk. Judith was standing at the window, looking out across the city.

'A project I'm working on.'

'Do you mind if I look?'

I shrugged indifference even though I was uneasy.

He studied each print for a while. Judith limped across, stood beside him, and leaned against him with one hand on his shoulder.

'I don't understand,' Alex said eventually. 'This is . . . landscaping.'

'I don't think of it as that.'

'It will be a sculpture?'

'It's his masterwork,' Judith said drily. 'It says so in the gallery leaflet.'

'It'll be a sculpture,' I agreed. 'I don't know what form it will take. The scale is large but restricted. When it's completed, perhaps people will think of it as architecture.'

Alex held one hand horizontally in the air. 'The land is flat?'

'Virtually. Apart from the hillock.'

He looked through the photographs again, concentrating on the mound. 'This is near the centre,' he observed.

'Coincidence.'

'It looks as if it has been deliberately placed there.'

'Maybe. And I may be responsible for having it levelled.'

He tilted the photographs and peered at them intently, as if they contained a hidden message which an alteration in perspective could make clear. As an adolescent I had squinted at a reproduction of Holbein's *Ambassadors* from just such an angle, so that the mysterious elongated shape towards the bottom edge of the picture was revealed as a skull. No doubt Alex had once done the same.

'You'll not find a *memento mori* hidden in there,' I warned him. 'There's no puzzle. It's just countryside.'

Alex pointed to the mound. 'This isn't a natural feature.'

'Maybe it is. You can't be expected to know about English topography. The last Ice Age didn't reach as far as Cyprus. It could be a drumlin – a mound of gravel left by a glacier. Or it could be a spoil heap from an ancient mine or the remains of a building for storing ice. The house is near enough.'

'Perhaps an expert will tell you it's a burial mound.'

'I don't think so.'

'A hill fort,' Judith suggested.

'It's too small. Look, I have someone checking it. Whatever it is, I'm certain that it's nothing important.'

'You'll tell us what you find out?' She asked.

Judith spoke as if we were about to seal a partnership. I had come to believe that I carried a vestigial responsibility for her welfare, and I intended to discharge this as efficiently as I could. Judith saw a different future. In it we exchanged discoveries, discussed projects, were thrillingly dependent on each other. Our relationship was more vivid than any affair, weightier, more charged. In her dreams we were not only united but, idealised.

'It could affect everything if this hillock was special in some way,' she continued eagerly. 'We'd like you to let us know – wouldn't we, Alex?'

'If it's worth telling you,' I said, 'I'll tell you.'

'Why did you have photographs taken from the air?' Alex asked.

'Setting. Proportion. I thought they may show up detail that wasn't visible on the ground.'

I looked again at the uppermost print. There was no solution in its groupings and shadings of grey; it could have been abstraction rather than topography.

I thought of a photograph taken by Man Ray. Years ago, when I had first seen it, I had been immediately fascinated by its oblique perspective, geometrical lines, and raised granular clumps. All these suggested that it was a solarised view of grassland and woods taken from an aeroplane. This was far from the truth. Ray had been a friend of Marcel Duchamp, who had been completing *The Bride Stripped Bare By Her Bachelors, Even*. Ray had taken a close-up of dust particles gathering on the incised glass surface. I often thought that his image had a kind of shared emphasis with my own work.

'You can climb to the top of the hill and look around,' Alex said.

'True; and I have done. But I like to have an aerial view.'

He turned to me with an interviewer's sharpness. 'Why? Because you're making something that can only be recognised from the air?'

I did not answer. He pressed me with an example.

'Like the drawings at Nazca?'

In Peru the desert at Nazca is like a draughtsman's pad. For thousands of square metres the ground is covered with abstract geometries and the outlines of insects, birds, reptiles, and even human figures.

'No,' I said, 'nothing like that. I have to work in three dimensions. And so many people know about Nazca that the idea would be too banal. Earthworks are much more interesting.'

Even as I spoke I began to think about a different plan. Perhaps it would be advantageous to retain the bulk of the Peermain mound and somehow sculpt it into a more pleasing form.

'Like Maiden Castle,' Alex suggested. 'I've been there,' he added proudly.

'I was thinking of some Native American earthworks. Like the Great Serpent Mound in Ohio. That shares a characteristic with Nazca. They can best be understood from the air.'

'I don't know that work,' he admitted, disappointment clouding his face.

'It's on one of Claire's postcards,' Judith advised him crisply. 'You should take a look at it.'

By now my imagination was racing with possibilities for the Peermain mound.

Rather than destroy it I could mould and shape it for my own ends. Or if for some reason it was important, historically or topographically, I could leave it unscathed and transform the land around it. When the trees had been felled I would have a tractor driven onto the collar of cleared earth that would surround the hill. That was when its metamorphosis would begin. My sculpture, my piece of England, might have to be of neither metal nor stone, but earth.

And its intricacies would not be fully noticed on the ground, where it might appear confusing, even maze-like. Its true shape, its clear, harmonious symmetries, could only be truly appreciated from the air.

I looked at Alex and then turned away.

He had shared something with me, and he did not even know it.

Surprisingly, our evening together was quite pleasant. We ate easily-prepared food taken from the freezer, and I opened a bottle of inexpensive but palatable wine. Like a suddenly attentive pupil, Alex asked questions about my contemporaries and about my own work. I answered them diplomatically, but I also turned the conversation to his boyhood in Cyprus and his knowledge of its culture. He was informed and eloquent about orthodox monasteries and Roman sites but scathing about the omnipresent busts of Makarios, which for him resembled totalitarian art.

He was at his most interesting, however, when he recalled visiting catacombs where supplicants left items of clothing jammed into crevices or tied around pillars. I remembered his description of Judith's squat; Alex had picked debris from the floor and placed it on higher levels, like a man acknowledging the presence of something that did not belong to the world of logic or sensation.

'You speak as if you still believe in God,' I said.

He waited for a moment before he answered; he was choosing his words carefully. 'I think that God is unlikely,' he said, 'but I also think that there are places in the world that can justifiably be called holy.'

'You don't think that's a contradiction?'

He shook his head. 'I don't,' he answered.

Judith's forwardness had deserted her. She was unusually quiet; merely to be in the house seemed to be enough. I found myself wondering what impressions or dreams were occupying her mind. Perhaps she was lost within conjecture, and was imagining a place for herself in the photographs on the wall.

When she and Alex had finished eating I put the plates in the dishwasher and turned it on, even though it was almost empty. I wanted no evidence left behind. Twice, or perhaps three times, I told them they would have to leave early in the morning because the cleaner arrived at nine.

'You've been very kind,' Judith said when the conversation began to lose impetus. Alex nodded his agreement. 'This has meant a lot to me,' she added.

'Right. But you must appreciate that you'll never be back here, ever.'

'I know. I've been trying to memorise things; trying to memorise the shell you live inside.' A faint smile played around her mouth.

Pointedly, I looked at my watch. 'Now I think it's time for bed,' I said.

It took me a few seconds to realise that I had spoken like a father addressing his child.

The night was harrowed by contradictory dreams. Only when they began to exhaust themselves did I lurch towards consciousness, jolting down from the high, unrelenting levels of imagination like a glider through layers of air until I found myself awake and hanging over the side of my bed.

The room was quiet and dark. Lillian's absence was like a physical hurt. I could not guess the time and my eyes were unable to focus on the clock's vivid green numerals. No matter how I tried they remained beyond sharpness and legibility. I realised that my breathing was much too shallow. Momentarily panicked, I struggled to sit up in bed while my lungs fought for their ease.

When my heart slowed the time become clear. It was just after two, the hour of the wolf, the time when children are born and adults die. I swung my legs to the floor. Although the terror of the dream had left its spoor in the room, everything was firm under my heels. I stood up and made my way to the bathroom.

I switched on the cruel light, stood at the lavatory and emptied my bladder. My urine was hot and smelled of ammonia. It was good to turn off the light and be surrounded by darkness again.

On the way back I hesitated and then, a burglar in my own home, I crept to the guest room door. The door was fractionally open, and even though the gap was no more than the razor-space between window-frames I could hear noises from inside.

Alex and Judith were making love. At this hour of the night one had woken the other; their need had been so sharp that they had been unable to wait until dawn.

I stood there for about a minute, intoxicated and repelled

by their pleasure, my mind's eye filled by tangled limbs and conjuctions of flesh.

I went back to bed and lay there. Claire's photograph hung in the darkness as if in a developing tray. I began to look forward to the morning when Judith and her lover would depart. After they had gone I would close the door on them, possibly for good. And then I would go back upstairs before the cleaner arrived and strip the sheets off the bed they had used. They would leave as much trace on the house as ghosts, but as with ghosts, I would always be aware that they had been present.

I couldn't sleep. Everything within me was keyed and alert. I found myself concentrating on the pattern of the overheard noises, on the architecture of the sighs shared by my daughter and her lover. I thought again of Angie, who had changed so much that I had not recognised her, whom I had denied for a second time.

A quarter of a century ago Angie had worked in a clothes shop and modelled part-time to earn enough money to buy mildly hallucinogenic drugs. For several weeks we had an affair that became increasingly violent in its passion. She clawed at me like a baited animal, often raising weals across my flesh which I did not hide from Eve. But Angie made me promise never to mark her own skin; she needed to be unblemished for her life class. Instead I put my hands on her face to blot out her senses other than the feel of my own body pressing into hers. On our last day together, she became so extreme that she dug sharpened fingernails into my back, and I in turn pressed my hands onto her mouth, blocking her breath until, when she broke away, she was gasping with pain and dizziness.

It was our last time together. When I went home later that day, Eve was lying on our bed in a room breathless with gas.

I never returned to Angie's flat. I never gave her a call. She, too, was sacrificed for the sake of my future. I had never seen her from that day until this, and I would never see her again, ever.

Unsettled by the day's events, and despairing of ever falling asleep, I decided to go downstairs. Although I promised myself not to pause again by the guest room door, I broke my promise.

Everything was quiet.

I went down the stairs brooding about what Judith had said about Alex's preoccupation with suffering. Perhaps he was a man who needed revenge; perhaps, after the murder of his father, he was unable to enter into any relationship that was not in some way marked by exploitation and controlled violence. Judith's thigh had been bruised the first time that I met her. Today she was supposed to have an injured ankle. And I could have been told a lie about the marks on her wrists. They had not looked like scars to me. It was possible that they were marks left after dangerous and frightening sexual games, games of suffering. Judith had told me confidently that my scratches would heal without scarring; possibly she knew exactly what she was talking about. Perhaps Alex was a liar and a mercenary. Perhaps he was like me as a young man; perhaps he needed his life to be changed.

For several minutes I stood under the kitchen light as if in the glare of an interrogation room, and then I walked across to the year planner. It was starred with a red sticker to show the date on which, contractually, I should have submitted final proposals for the estate sculpture. That had been a week ago. In three days I was due to meet Ken Takama. It was obvious what he was going to ask me.

My attention drifted to the surround of Claire's American postcards, and I looked again at the two in the lower right-hand corner of the planner.

In a winter landscape of earth and bare trees, a long, sinuous hill revealed itself as snake, more than a thousand feet long, with jaws gaping around a circular enclosure of some kind, possibly a stylised egg; the Serpent Mound State Memorial. Next to it, its eerily perfect dome as white as icing sugar, was the astronomical Observatory at Mount Palomar.

I went to the study and looked at the bookshelves. Among the exhibition catalogues, the volumes of high-quality reproductions, the cultural histories and biographies, there was a book of photographs taken from the air. I picked it from the shelf, went back upstairs and lay in bed turning the pages, hoping that it would be a whetstone for my imagination.

I opened it at random and saw the zoo with its mesh-tent aviary where Judith and I had spent our first meeting. I turned over quickly. Here were the huge geometries of the Egyptian pyramids, which had once been covered with a thin skin of fine white limestone so that they blazed white in the sunlight. I turned more pages. Here were the labyrinthine complexities of Nazca, the monumental basilicas and domes of European cathedrals and Arabian mosques, the truncated cone of the Herodeion, the hemispherical storehouses for rice in Mali, the ramparts and ditches of Offa's Dyke and Maiden Castle, the strange unearthly loops and humpbacks of American theme parks.

And I began to think about the mound, *my* mound, rising from its surrounding wood, shining into the next century and the centuries that followed it like a cold, pure beacon of truth.

5

I had not planned to visit the cemetery, but as I drove towards the Peermain estate I remembered how, a few short months ago, I had become a mourner for a man I did not know. Terry Evans was the kind of person who would remind me of such an accident of fate; what had been mere coincidence for me would have greater significance for him. It would be politic, I decided, to see the grave.

I parked the car and walked between the black cast-iron gates. I could clearly remember the route the cortège had taken, so I followed the path to the grave without difficulty.

When I came to the plot I realised that, against all indications, I had thoughtlessly assumed I would find flowers. There were none. The squares of relaid turf were bare, with their cut edges growing together like sutures. No one had left any offerings here; the grave had remained unvisited. On the grey headstone the names of the wife and daughter seemed to have dimmed further, as if they were being consumed by fog, but Archie Sproat's name shone as if it had been incised and painted onto the marble that very morning.

Forty years. He had been on his own for a long time. I waited for less than a minute before I walked away.

A short while later I drew up at the vicarage. Terry's wife

led me to his study and left us alone. I sat in a mahogany chair with a worn leather seat while Terry sat behind his desk and smoothed his hair with a curious, dandyish motion. On the bookshelf behind him were volumes of Bible commentary, concordances, and British history, but only one that concerned itself with art, and that was an overview of Western civilisation. There were also two dozen or more books of theology and philosophy, including two on his beloved Berkeley.

For several minutes Terry insisted on nothing but small talk, and I noticed that he showed faint traces of a smirk as one bland generalisation followed on from another. He was playing with me.

Eventually impatience made me cut across his musings. 'You told me you had a photocopy for me. I assumed it was something important.'

'That's true.'

'Well?'

'A friend made it. He has all the original journals in an unbroken sequence. They go back to the end of the last century. That's where the information comes from.'

'Whose journals?'

He looked surprised. 'Did I not say? Why, the Antiquarian and Archaeological Society, of course. My friend, you know, has a particular interest in paleolithic and neolithic sites.'

I had convinced myself that the hillock was unimportant. Now my imagination bolted like a panicked mare – the mound was a barrow, after all; it had been known to the Victorians, and now Terry's old university wanted to excavate it; there was talk of it being an important national treasure. The possibilities jostled and fought in my mind.

'You know, they were exhaustive indexers in those days,' Terry went on, 'so it wasn't a time-consuming task. I asked him if he minded photocopying the page. He said he didn't.'

'How bad is it?'

Terry could not keep the smile off his face as he handed me two sheets of paper. I took them from him. Irregular carbon-black borders framed the text; the original had not been laid symmetrically on the copier glass.

On each page were paragraphs of small news items – a Bronze Age pot donated to a local museum, a few Roman coins discovered in a field near the county border. I saw nothing to do with the estate or the mound until I chanced on the name of Peermain under the title *A Disappointing Investigation*.

Although it began on one page and finished on the next, the account was only a few hundred words long. It reported the efforts of two Gentleman Antiquaries who had dug into the mound on the Peermain estate. The investigation had been carried out with the approval of the Peermain family, whose personal papers apparently contained no mention of the hill. The antiquaries had taken cores from its entire depth, and also sunk probes into its sides, finding nothing but soil and a variety of stone, some of it obviously placed as supports. None of this stone was stacked in barrow, kiln or motte configurations.

I looked at Terry. He sat with his fingertips touching, like a complacent teacher.

'It's not ancient?'

'The last paragraph,' he said.

I read on. The authors' conclusion was that although the mound resembled an ancient barrow, thorough investigation had now shown that it was an artificial earthwork of much more recent origin, obviously erected to provide the most effective panorama across the surrounding countryside. The authors suggested that although it could have been built as early as the sixteenth century, it probably dated from the eighteenth, when several nearby houses had also built artificial hills for belvederes. Since there was no evidence of any construction on the summit of the earthwork, their conclusion was that the builder's original intention had been abandoned.

I could feel the tension uncoiling and, at the same time, a sense of excitement began to warm me. At last my ideas could begin to take a workable shape.

'A belvedere?' I asked.

'A pavilion, a folly, a secular temple. They were all the rage about two hundred and fifty years ago. The owners of every country house felt they had to have one. Because belvederes had to command an aesthetically satisfying view, they were built on mounds constructed especially for the purpose. According to my friend, often just the mound was completed; the gentry would stroll to the summit to admire their lands. Hillocks like yours are all over England. Apparently it's easy to mistake them for something a lot older.'

Triumph tightened my hands into fists. I had a brief, satisfying vision of labourers taking their ease on the summit of the newly-built hill, smoke curling upwards from the bowls of their clay pipes. They would have had every justification to be pleased with their work. Perhaps there had even been a kind of ironic ceremony, with ritually broken pipes and spilled wine as a libation for the mound.

'Your colleague knew it was recent?' I asked.

'All the time.'

'There's no doubt?'

'None. You know, when you think about it, your little hill is much more likely to be a rich person's folly than an ancient burial site. We should have realised that when we discussed it. We speculated so much that we missed the obvious.'

Terry paused for a moment, tilted his head on one side like an intelligent dog, and went on.

'In Berkeley's *Principles* he comments that first of all

we raise clouds of dust, and then we complain that we can't see.'

'So it's not even a folly. It's just a mound. Something abandoned and unimportant. They never got as far as laying the foundations for the actual folly.'

I read the report again.

'*A Disappointing Investigation,*' I said after a while. 'But not for me. I'm grateful to you, Terry. Maybe you'd like to see the mound when the trees are down?'

I saw him turning over replies in his mind.

'Whatever happens, surveyors will have to check it,' I went on. 'They'll be able to confirm this report. I'll ask Ken Takama if you can be there. It would be appropriate, don't you think?'

'You're happy that you're destroying something that's only two hundred and fifty years old, and not four thousand?'

'I thought about having it bulldozed level, but now I don't think I'll do that. I'm not certain of the final shape the land will take, but I'll transform it in some way.'

'You're still going to destroy it.'

'Culture's worth a little destruction. We both know that's true.'

'You don't seriously expect me to agree with you.'

'Perhaps not. I only know that art advances over art that has gone before it.'

He withdrew his fingers from each other as if they had become gummed together, paused, then joined them again.

'You're a decent, humane man, Jamie. And yet you pretend there's a part of you which is selfish and mercenary, and has no feeling at all other than feeling for what you create. You know, I think that may be one of the reasons why I find you interesting.'

I would not be drawn, and smiled my most tolerant smile.

'You have no evidence that I'm decent and humane. You don't know what I've done in my past.'

'The past? That's no concern of mine. St Augustine said that there is no good man who has not, once in his life, been bad. I prefer to think of people as I see them in the present. And you, Jamie, have lived a happily married life for a long time now. Few people do that these days, especially not in your line of business. And you followed Archie Sproat's coffin when no one else would. It was an act of kindness you needn't have made.'

'That was pure chance.'

'You know, I don't think that's the case. Not at all.'

'Perhaps if I'd known more about him I wouldn't have done it. I would have been like everyone else. I can't say I would be automatically sympathetic to a recluse. Was there no family at all?'

'There was only one daughter.'

'The dead one?'

He nodded. 'Of course it happened before I was even born. I was told all about it by the previous vicar. No doubt, in time, I'll pass on the tale to my successor. It's a sad and disturbing story. One might say it was something of a parable. Certainly it contains a lesson about misjudgement.'

'Why? What happened?'

'The girl was abducted.'

'And murdered?'

'It was a terrible, terrible case. She was only a child.'

I thought of Grace, lying in her cot with her eyes open while her mother lay dead in the next room.

'There's no exact date of death,' I said.

'You've been back to the grave, haven't you? I knew you would. I much prefer your humane side, Jamie.'

'Go on.'

'Everyone assumed that the girl was killed shortly after

she was kidnapped. It was more comforting for the Sproats to think that. Of course, they never knew the actual date.'

'Who did it?'

Terry shook his head.

'No one knows?' I asked. 'They never found anyone?'

'In such cases suspicion often falls on the parents.'

'But it wasn't them. It can't have been.'

'Of course it wasn't. But it took more than a year for the girl's body to be found, and when it was, it was discovered a hundred miles away. The Sproats couldn't have travelled such a distance and returned to their home in such a short time; it was impossible. From the very start a whispering campaign had been carried on against them, and by the time the body was found local suspicions had been given free rein for more than twelve months. Both Archie Sproat and his wife were reviled and despised. Some even doubted that the body was the right girl. You see, hatred had built up to such a pitch that no one could admit that they'd been wrong. And the Sproats testified that under her clothing their daughter was wearing a small gold locket in the shape of a heart. That was never found. Hardly a surprise – the murderer must have thrown it away or sold it. But it was enough to condemn the Sproats for the rest of their lives.'

Terry sat ruminatively for a few seconds before speaking again.

'She was identified by her shoes. There was nothing else left of her, I understand.'

'I see.'

'Frightening, isn't it? It must have taken weeks or months to go through all the legal procedures. Eventually she was buried; she was the first one in the family grave. I imagine that no one went to the funeral except the parents, officials, the police. The mother joined her daughter just a short while later. The poor woman probably wanted to die.'

'And her husband lived for another forty years.'

'On his own, mistrusted and feared, refusing to see those who wanted to help.'

'Like you?'

'Quite.'

A quarter of a century ago I had picked up my daughter's carrycot and taken it into the living room. Grace watched me silently all the time. If she had been older, capable of knowledge, I would have sworn that her unblinking stare was a condemnation or a curse. But I was still alive, and had prospered.

'When the grave was opened for Archie Sproat and I stood at its edge,' Terry went on, 'I was filled with a sense of failure. There are times in anyone's life when they feel they have failed a test. But you weren't to know what had happened. What did you feel?'

I looked at him and then looked away. He was staring at me as if he was trying to penetrate my memories.

'I was thinking about my breakthrough as an artist,' I confessed.

'I don't think so.'

'It's true. The pieces that made my reputation were slots of reinforced concrete set into a hillside. Some people saw them as petrified graves.'

'And you weren't curious about the man we were burying? You had no thoughts for him at all? I don't believe you.'

'Terry, all I know is what you tell me. I have nothing to do with the Sproats. Nothing.'

'You were the only one who followed Archie's coffin who was not an official. Don't you think that puts you in a special position? God works in complex and mysterious ways, Jamie. The only thing we can be certain of is that eventually we'll all be called to account. I don't know why you were late for that meeting . . .'

'I told you, I wasn't well.'

'. . . but if you hadn't been, you would never have followed us to the graveside. Was that just coincidence, do you think? Was it mere chance that you were late?'

I folded the photocopies and slid them into my pocket. 'That's right, Terry. It was just chance.'

But as I drove away I brooded on the workings of the thing we called chance. The Sproats had lost their daughter, but I still had mine. Their anguish was deepened by uncertainty and delay, and made unbearable by false accusation. Eventually, after more than a year, they found that nothing could ever be known about when their little girl died, or how. She was beyond the most elementary recognition; even an identifying locket had been stolen. Her only individuality rested in a pair of shoes, and they must have been the same as hundreds of other children would have worn.

And the Sproats' agony did not abate. From the moment of their child's abduction they lived in a torture garden of recrimination, ostracism, and perhaps worst of all, imagination.

When I reached the village I found a small florist's. I stared indecisively at the blooms for several minutes before eventually buying a bunch of red tulips which the assistant put in a cellophane wrapper for me. Back in the car I laid them on the passenger seat. Then I wrote my name and Judith's on a plain white card and tied it to the stems. On my way back I would stop at the cemetery and leave the flowers on the Sproat grave.

I had not decided this without first considering what I would do if Terry Evans were ever to mention to me that he had seen the flowers. I already had an answer to the question that would be uppermost in his mind; Judith Ford was an old student of mine. If he nodded understandingly, I would elaborate my lie; she had been moved when I had told her of Archie Sproat's lonely funeral. I had added her name as an afterthought, and as a kind of proof that strangers other than myself had been affected by the Sproat family tragedy.

I was convinced that if I were to tell Terry the truth about Judith he would congratulate me on having been allowed a second chance. We are creatures of false judgement, he would say, forever confusing ourselves, forever complaining that we cannot see the truth. And he would ask me about Lillian, and counsel me to be brave enough to admit my errors to her.

It was impossible. Once, a long time ago when my life with her was still taking its pattern, I had considered making a confession to Lillian. But the moment had passed and each day buried it deeper. Now it was lost, irrecoverable beneath an accumulation of habit and time.

But even if I had confessed to either Lillian or Terry, even if I had been foolish enough to tell something approaching the truth, I could never reveal what had happened after I found Eve.

She was dead, or as near to death as made no difference; I had felt her unsupported weight as I dragged her from the bed. She lay on the floor, her arms by her sides and her legs slightly apart, her last unread message left beside the bed. The smell of the gas was lessening, and everyday, unthreatening city noises drifted in through the open windows – cars driving along the road, someone arguing in the street, a record being played behind open windows in another building, the humming roar of an aeroplane descending to the distant airport.

I leaned against the wall and trembled, but it was with anticipation. After the shock and the horror I was buoyed up by an unexpected flood of elation. It seemed to me that Eve's suicide offered me a new chance, and I felt like a man whose sentence has been lifted and who can at last walk out into a richer world. Only Grace was in the way.

After two or three minutes I closed the windows again.

I found a pair of gloves, put them on my hands, and walked to the door of the larder. Fixed to it was a sheet of paper. Written on it were the words *Open This Door First; Grace Is In Here*. I tore the message from the door, folded it, and put it into my shirt pocket. Then I lifted the adhesive tape from around the frame. It came away from the wood with the noise of a file rasping metal.

At first I thought Grace was asleep, but as I lifted the carrycot from its collapsible stand her eyes opened. They seemed to be perfect in their shape and colour, and I did my best not to look at them.

I put the cot on the floor beside Eve and then replaced the tape around the door. All the time I was aware that I was being watched; I would not have thought a child's dumb silence could be so accusatory.

I turned the gas taps back on. Their hiss began to smother the room. I turned to go. Perhaps by accident, perhaps of necessity, I was suddenly trapped by my daughter's motionless stare.

Absurdly, unnecessarily, I wanted to say something. I wanted to justify myself to a child who would not understand a word I said, and who would die quietly, without pain, and leave behind a world which did not want her.

I was strong enough to say nothing, and walked out of the door and closed it behind me. I got as far as locking it and descending the first flight of stairs before guilt terrified me and I sprang back up the steps.

The room was sickly with gas, but Grace was still wide-eyed, her stare still as blinkless as an infant god's.

I kept myself from looking at her as I turned off the taps and opened the windows.

*   *   *

I expected that several of Ken Takama's colleagues would join us for lunch, but there were only two of us to sit opposite each other in the large, newly-renovated dining room with its oak panelling and silverware. There was even a small typewritten menu of standardised Japanese foods and French wine. As soon as I looked at it I realised that there were too many courses; the meal was designed both to impress and intimidate.

I commented on the generosity of the hospitality, and said that it must be expensive to have such food prepared merely for us. Ken pretended that the company's European chef wished to perfect his oriental cuisine. I smiled and nodded, but was sharply aware that I was being flattered, either to be coaxed or dismissed. I made small talk as a delaying tactic, even stealing some of Terry Evans's anodyne generalisations. I was certain that Ken's unstated purpose was to quiz me on my plans for the commission.

Chance had made today the worst of all days to be questioned. I did not know what I should worry about, or what I should feel. All the time I thought of Judith, and yet I was unable to speak about her. I was like a creature from mythology, doomed to carry the burden of her memory until the day I died.

Ken was evasive while we ate nori-maki, but when we were served with the tiny dishes of chicken with prawns he began to detail the success of the company and say how proud and honoured he was to work for it. He had no need to tell me this; he knew I followed its fortunes with great interest. Nevertheless, as he lifted morsels with his personalised chopsticks, he insisted on quoting several international projects which he believed supported his case. When at last he paused it was to allow me to agree, so I dutifully complied. I did this without hesitation; it was usually politic to sweeten Ken with a drip-feed of reassurance.

Midway through the steamed rice, azuki beans and sesame seeds he unexpectedly pointed a stubby finger at the painstaking reproduction of Gainsborough's *Mr and Mrs Peermain* hanging above the huge empty fireplace.

'Perhaps one of these days we'll be able to have the original there,' he said.

He gave me no time to demur, and continued.

'Like the Greeks, Jamie, our company believes that art has a definite geographical place. The subjects of that painting are the man who commissioned it and his wife. And this room is where it hung until the middle of the last century.'

'You'll never get the original canvas,' I said.

'No?'

'Times have changed too much. Patronage and exclusiveness have been replaced by museum culture and cheap reproductions.'

'Jamie, you would have no living if that was all there was. It's companies like ours, benefactors like us, who enable you to live a good life.'

I lifted my glass to give him a half-mocking toast and then studied the painting again.

The easel must have been set up where the conifers had since been planted, on the estate side of the wall behind Terry's church. Peermain stood next to a rustic fence in his green frock-coat. A flintlock was tucked casually under one arm, two retrievers with eager slack tongues sat by his boots, and his languid watery eyes looked down from the picture and out into the centuries since his death. Beside him his wife, pretty as a playing-card design, sat on a rustic wooden seat in a motionless splash of white frills and lace. Behind them stretched their grassy rich leagues with, far enough away to give a golden proportion between building and countryside, the house we were now sitting inside. Off to the right, in a tiny detail I had never noticed before, was a grassy mound that nowadays barely thrust its head above a surrounding ring of trees.

'There's a famous argument about this work,' I said.

'Yes. Two famous English critics disagreed.'

'Right. One said the Peermains were contemplating nature. The other said they were contemplating property.'

'I read about it some weeks ago, in the draft of part of our book on the history of the estate. Our writer has turned out to be an excellent researcher, well ahead of the schedule we agreed. You, of course, are well behind yours.'

Before I could respond Ken began to speak again.

'I take no sides in the debate on this painting's meaning. There's never any true agreement in art. Some say we promote your work because of its cultural worth. Others say we do it merely as an investment.'

'I know. And you've never told me what the truth is.'

He leaned back, his chopsticks held like pincers.

'The truth? Of course you know what the truth is; you've worked with our company for a long time.' He paused, and added slyly, 'What do you think it is?'

'You do both; that's the truth.'

Ken's smile always seemed private. I went on.

'Your company likes the fame that someone like me brings with him. Why? Because you don't want to be seen as an economic machine and nothing more. You want to be socially aware, environmentally friendly, culturally alert. Commission work from me, or from someone with my reputation, and you legitimise your liberal, concerned, adventurous image. And you're also storing assets. Over the past twenty years multinationals have all begun to use art as an investment opportunity. Van Gogh's *Sunflowers*, for instance.'

'But we're slightly different.'

He tilted his head on the word *slightly*, so that he studied me from a stalker's angle.

'I've said that we believe that art has a definite place. Your work is a fixed part of this estate. It can't be taken away like the Gainsborough. We can't ship it to an auction house and turn it into cash.'

'No.'

'Whatever you do, we must live with it. Although legally, of course, we could destroy it.'

I looked at him, momentarily shocked, and again he smiled his inaccessible little smile.

'Legally,' I repeated.

He nodded.

'But you wouldn't do that. It would contradict—'

He held up a hand to silence me. 'Quite. So we operate on mutual trust. We must do. You agree?'

'What are you getting at, Ken?'

The waiter appeared by our side but Ken shook his head. 'Give us three minutes,' he said sharply. The waiter retreated behind the door into the kitchen and watched us glumly though its circle of glass.

Ken shifted his weight and leaned back a little. 'I'm having some pressure put on me. From above. You can hardly be surprised. They want you to produce something definite for us. A plan, a sketch, a maquette, something of that nature. To show good faith.'

'I see.'

'And then there's the matter of the hill.'

'What about it?'

Again he did not answer me directly, but instead began to talk about the company's plans for the publication of the Peermain book. Copies would be available by the end of the year, and would be handed out as gifts or mementoes to official guests who stayed at the house – although I, of course, would also receive a copy. The Gainsborough portrait would be on the cover, and one or two of my Interlocking Pieces would be shown inside.

'Ken, why don't you just tell me you'd like the commission finished by the time the book comes out?'

'It would be helpful. Of course, if you're agreeable, we could incorporate one or two aerial photographs of the work as it progresses. As we agreed, you wouldn't be restricted from publishing those photographs yourself – whenever you decide to have another book of your own published.'

'And what exactly do you want to say about the hill?'

'You were talking of having it levelled.'

'I don't think so,' I lied.

He was puzzled. My contradiction had thrown him.

'Re-shaped,' I corrected him, 'not levelled.'

'That isn't what you said.'

'Wasn't it?'

'I'm quite clear about it.'

I laughed; it was meant to be disarming.

'I'm sorry, Ken; I do get a little excitable at times. No, I don't want the mound flattened. I intend to use it. Apart from anything else, it was specially built. Did you know?'

'Our writer told me it was probably artificial.'

'Built as a vantage, a look-out, two hundred or so years ago. Did she know that?'

There was a slight pause before he replied. 'She said it might be important.'

'It's not. It was the first stage of a plan that failed. The idea was to construct a pavilion where the Peermains and their lordly friends could admire the view. But for some reason or another they never got round to completing it. So we have the mound but no pavilion, no . . . observatory.'

The last word began to chime in my mind before I spoke it. I thought of Alex speculating on how the site would look when viewed from a thousand feet; I thought of watchers staring, not out across the parkland, but up into the sky.

'Gambling debts,' he mused.

'What?'

'One of the Peermains was notoriously profligate. I was reading about him only the other night. He may not have been able to afford a pavilion. You're certain that's what the hill was meant for?'

'Completely. Terry Evans did some research for me. I think he'd like to be here when the surveyors go over the mound. I'll need surveyors just to test its structure.'

Ken nodded. 'Yes, I understand. But we don't want to act like barbarians.'

'Of course not.'

'And I think we would want something which honoured the spirit of the original intention.'

'What you'll get,' I said carefully, 'is a late twentieth-century postmodernist variant on the original concept.'

He gave a small grunt of satisfaction and leaned further backwards, eager to relish my invention. I continued.

'The original plan must have been to build a neo-classical arbour with a dome and pillars, similar to those in Claude's mythological landscapes. It would be absurd and anachronistic to build such a thing now. Instead we have a chance of making something that will serve the same purpose, and yet be a completely independent work of sculpture.'

Even as I spoke my vision had begun to clear. Elements of the new work lay strewn and unrecognised around my imagination. For a long time they had all been within my reach. Now I could identify them, gather them, begin to fit them more closely together.

'The Peermains would have employed an architect, not a sculptor,' Ken objected.

As I began to reply, I felt myself become infected by the very excitement that I was trying to generate. I was thinking of domes, of vaulting, of cathedrals. Then, unexpectedly, I thought of Alex recalling the catacombs he had visited as a child, and how patterns he had followed then had carried over into his adult life.

'This will transcend divisions, Ken. It will be accessible yet mysterious, decorative yet functional. I want to attract the discriminating individual, not the unthinking crowd. For those who come to it in the right frame of mind, it will offer an insight which might be described as religious.'

The word startled him. 'Religious?'

I retreated. 'Not in the doctrinal sense.'

'In what sense, then?'

'Mystery. Affirmation. Wholeness.'

'I see,' he said, and beckoned to the waiter to begin serving the next course. His moment of doubt had passed. The kitchen door swung open as quickly as a reflex. 'I had no doubt that you had an idea. And I appreciate that you're always unwilling to talk about such ideas until they've begun to mature.'

'It's just the way I work,' I agreed.

The waiter served us each with a small fried mackerel marinated in rice wine and soya sauce. I did not think I could eat any more, but Ken began to systematically separate the flesh as if he had eaten nothing else.

'Forgive me, Jamie – I have to be able to tell my colleagues something more tangible about your scheme.'

'I don't have a plan or a model yet.'

'Then tell me more about the idea. Abstraction is no good; I need to be able to talk about what the finished work will look like.'

And, like an apparition gradually taking on detail, an image of the transformed land began to take shape in my mind.

'I'll get your team to clear the wood in an oval shape around the hillock. The central area will be restored to something resembling the original intended shape, but the remaining trees will screen it from the parkland. Approaching it will be like entering something mythic and elemental; a kind of sacred grove.'

'I understand.'

'I'll have the ground dug in deep concentric furrows, either three or four, like siege fortifications. Obviously it will take a while to clear the roots and stones – and we'll have to arrange for a temporary path through the wood that will be wide enough to let logging equipment through. The furrows will have to be deep enough to be impassable, because they'll serve as a stylised ditches, like the ditches dug to heighten the ramparts of iron age forts, or the protective circles around some megaliths. After the banks have been stabilised the ditches will be coated white, perhaps with veined quartz. A visitor will feel contradictory sensations—'

'Mystery and wholeness,' Ken repeated without conviction.

'Yes, but you missed out affirmation. And I think, too, they'll encounter a kind of enigmatic purity.'

He grimaced slightly. 'Try to keep it visual, Jamie.'

'A thin pathway, wide enough for just one person, will lead down the bank into the bottom of the first ditch and then burrow through the ramparts until it reaches the edge of the mound.'

'One person? Only one?'

'Right. I'm an artist, not a populist. It's no use pretending that my work is accessible to a wide range of people – it isn't. I'm only interested in those who are willing to surrender to it and not ask too many questions.'

'And the mound?'

'That will be dressed with highly reflective white stone – the best marble, if the budget can take it.'

He shrugged. 'Maybe.'

'If the finished mound resembles anything, it will resemble an observatory dome. We'll have steps up the side, or perhaps just handholds and footholds. There will be room for one person, and only one, to stand on the flattened top. The summit will be so sparkling, so crystalline, that when the sun shines it will blaze as white as a beacon. And whoever stands there will be able to look out towards the house, and back towards the church, and away across the fields, just as was originally intended. And at night it will be a perfect place to stand and watch the stars crawl across the sky.'

I said nothing for a few seconds, but studied Ken's opaque features as he finished eating the mackerel. Apart from the first few mouthfuls I had hardly touched mine.

'From the air,' he ruminated, 'do you know what your pale ditches and white dome would look like?'

'Tell me.'

'An eye,' he said. 'A gigantic eye staring upwards.'

The skin tightened across my cheekbones, and for a brief illusory moment my nostrils were full of gas.

'Is that not deliberate?' he asked.

I shook my head.

'Are you sure?'

I cleared my throat. 'My work has different resonances for different people. Each observer brings his or her own interpretation to it.'

'Confess it, Jamie; the resemblance is deliberate. It's too obvious not to be. A camera looking straight down would clearly see a single eye staring back. Perhaps without realising it you were thinking of ancient civilisations. Think of gigantic statues of gods that archaeologists dug out of sand. After all, you've been very articulate in announcing that you want the mound to have a divine quality.'

'You think of it in terms of an eye. Others wouldn't. What about your author? Perhaps she would only see abstractions, geometries.'

'She may see more clearly than me, you mean? I don't think so. She's an academic, an archivist, very far removed from the mystery and wonder that you want to create. For instance, she finds your Interlocking Pieces flippant, a kind of diversion, but that's all.'

'Condemned out of her own mouth. But she'll still put them in the book – won't she?'

'As well as your new work, just as we agreed. Don't concern yourself, Jamie. She's much more interested in the rise and fall of the Peermains than in your activities. After all, that's her job.'

I allowed myself a small touch of sarcasm. 'Then she's little more than a glorified journalist, and perhaps not a very thorough one. She should have been able to tell you about the origin of the mound, but she couldn't.'

'She would have found out sooner or later. At the moment she's spending a good deal of time on the claimant. It's a fascinating story, but there's an entire case to read.'

He laid down his chopsticks, picked up a napkin, and wiped a thin film of fish oil from his lips. As he placed his fingers around his wineglass he noticed my plate.

'Are you no longer hungry, Jamie?'

'I'm fine, thanks,' I said, but any lingering appetite had vanished.

This time it was Ken who raised his glass to me. 'I'm grateful for your candour about the new project. We should drink to its success.'

'Yes,' I agreed quietly, 'let's do that.'

Something was worrying at me and would not let me rest. It was without recognisable shape, but already I was beginning to sense its frightening power.

I put my glass back on the table but misjudged it so that the wine spilled over its side. A stain widened across the tablecloth.

'The claimant?' I asked, my voice suddenly brittle.

'That's right. Some date the family's decline from that time.'

'What claimant?'

'It's a very famous case. Our writer is very excited by the puzzle.'

'I don't know about any puzzle.'

'The man was Australian. He said he had forgotten who he was until, by chance, he read about the Peermains' search. His memory returned and he realised that he was the one they were looking for. Some believed him.'

And I felt again the sensation of hanging on to a rail while my toppling ship slid unstoppably into a black, engulfing sea.

'What happened?' I asked, and was not even certain that I succeeded in speaking the last word.

'Ah,' Ken said. It was a small, appreciative noise, as if he were a raconteur at last allowed to hold an audience. 'In the middle of the nineteenth century the Peermains' eldest son took a ship bound for Australia. It never arrived. The vessel was declared lost, its crew and passengers given up for dead. No survivors were ever found.'

'Until the Peermain boy turned up?'

'Ten years later a man walked into a newspaper office in Sydney and said he was the heir to the Peermain fortune. He told an improbable story about being the only survivor of a wreck off the coast, of being rescued and looked after by Aborigines, of losing his memory for years. Money was raised on his behalf so that he could sail to England and claim his inheritance. He came to this house. Probably he sat in this room. Some of the family said he was an impostor; others said they recognised him as the missing boy grown to manhood. There was a court case that was the talk of Britain and the world. It must have been like Anna Anderson's claim that she was the Princess Anastasia – conflicting evidence, the family and the country divided, sinister pressure groups at work behind the scenes.'

'How do you know he was an impostor?'

Ken pointed to the Gainsborough. Peermain's watery eyes, unchanged over the centuries, stared down at us.

'He looked nothing like that, even though some people fooled themselves into thinking that he did.'

'Physical resemblance isn't everything.'

'But some saw just such a resemblance. That's the real puzzle – why some of the Peermains were eager to accept such obvious deceit. Everything about the man was wrong – his height, his accent, his recollections.'

'He could have been genuine.'

'He was an impostor. No doubt about it. As the case neared its end the truth came out. The man was the son of parents raised in this part of England. Perhaps they even poached on this estate. But they were transported to Australia before their son was born. No doubt they told him all about their youth. The rest he could pick up from newspaper articles and from people in the know who wished him to succeed. He had backers; there may have been a conspiracy to defraud. Wisely, the man disappeared before the formal verdict. No one knows what happened to him. He probably ended his days where he began them, in the outback, with the next person living miles away.'

Ken looked up at me and his expression stiffened.

'Are you all right, Jamie? You've gone very pale.'

I tried to say that I was fine, but my mouth opened and no sound came out.

Ken stood up quickly. The chairlegs squealed on the floor.

'A doctor,' he said; 'I'll get a doctor.'

I shook my head and managed to speak. 'It's nothing,' I said, 'I'll be okay in a couple of minutes. Pour me a glass of water and I'll be all right.'

But I felt that my very bones had grown too weak to

hold my body, and the breath rasped in my throat as if every ounce of oxygen were being drawn out of the air.

Thirty minutes later I parked my car beside the black gates of the cemetery and lifted the bunch of red tulips from the passenger seat. I walked to the grave in a turmoil of conflicting emotions. I was stalled by doubt, plunged with dizzying velocity into fury, lifted by relief.

I had to find a victim other than myself. I was desperate for a culprit who could take the blame for my naïve and uncritical trust. A dark cloud began to curtain the sun. Its shadow edged steadily across the mown grass and dulled the names of the dead.

I placed the tulips at the centre of the squares of turf on the Sproats' grave. They looked like petals of blood against the green. A chill settled through the air. I stood with my hands linked in front of me like a priest.

If I had been able to believe in God I might have prayed for the Sproats and their damaged souls, and then given thanks that the scales had been taken from my own eyes. But I had never experienced the luxury of religious belief. Even the way I stood was self-conscious, like a parody. I unlaced my fingers, folded my arms and stepped back.

It was Archie Sproat who was to blame for my plight. He had misled me. His pathetic life had sensitised me, stripped wisdom from my thoughts, thrown it aside. His tragedy had forced me to dwell on my own loss. And because he had been unjustly condemned, he had encouraged me to think of my own moral salvation.

I wanted to snatch up the tulips and flail them across his gravestone. I wanted to rip the petals, pulp the stems, let sap trickle like spittle across his name and the names of his wife and daughter. Only a lurching sense of control, and perhaps a kind of residual decorum, prevented me from doing this.

Since my boyhood I had been suggestible, both in my art and in life. Comments by friends, other artists' work, natural forms had been at the root of all my completed pieces. Even the plan I had sketched for Ken Takama was both a composite of familiar objects and a transformation of them. And I had begun to dwell on those objects because of a pattern of apparently unconnected events – postcards from America, a discussion on the origin of the mound, remarks hazarded by Alex Stylianou, a volume of aerial photographs.

I had never denied – at least not to myself – that my best work arose from good fortune, but I could not accept that it was a product of mere chance. Instead I was convinced that there must be something, a grand unknowable order of fate, that enabled me to summon the right images at the right time, that perhaps even encouraged people to say the right things to me.

Over the years I had become convinced that this also applied to my own life. I accumulated good luck as a magnet attracts metal. An alchemist, alert to the transmutation of souls as well as objects, would have seen that I was graced by fortune, brushed by glamour.

This was why I had been unable to rid myself of the greatest threat to my equilibrium, affluence, ease. Judith Ford had insinuated herself into my life; she had even slept in my own house. Without fully realising it, I had begun to believe that she, too, was part of an unrecognised pattern. Her return was one of a number of events that were not discrete but linked, not accidental but triggered – the newspaper profile, the loss of the Sproat girl, the appearance of Alex, even my meeting with Angie.

So I had begun to accept that I was right to tolerate Judith, even to welcome her. Once again the processes of fate had been engineered to my advantage. Alex, unaware of what he was doing, had inched me towards a resolution of the Peermain commission. Everything had appeared to be working for the best result. In the end, I thought, perhaps we would all be rewarded.

I stepped further away from the grave and looked round the deserted cemetery. The sky was full of broken cloud, and the tips of the yews swayed a little in the breeze.

Now I knew that there was another possibility. And the more I considered it, the more probable it seemed.

I had allowed myself to be duped, not only by Judith and Alex, but by a formless mosaic of events and coincidence. Faced with the random and unconnected I had conjured them into a pattern. That pattern was as illusory as the aerial view suggested by a photographer's close-up of dust gathering on the glass surface of a work of art. Like a spectator examining one of my own sculptures, I had reached conclusions that were false, unjustified, naïve.

And now I began to think that there could, after all, be a link between the Sproats' life and my own. It was something to do with misjudgement. We had each been the victims of forces outside our control. We shared a kind of innocence.

If good fortune had been at work, it had been within the story of the claimant. Ken Takama had had no need to tell me it; I might even have ignored his first casual reference to the case. Files in an archive told the true story. It was brought to Ken's attention, and then mine. An archivist's knowledge had clarified the nature of the mound. Perhaps Alex, too, had searched an archive, one I had not yet been able to raid. Perhaps he had found the article from half a lifetime ago, naming me, naming Eve, naming Grace.

Ignorance, prejudice and a missing locket had been enough to condemn the Sproats. Fame, and two articles printed a quarter of a century apart, had been enough for me to be subjected to this term of trial.

I looked around again. The sun had come out, but I still was not ready to leave.

The Sproats' accusers had refused to recognise the truth, despite the evidence. Judith had provided me with none. There was a resemblance to Eve which I now believed to be spurious. She had quoted me details from a birth certificate, that was all. Everything else could have been invented. Even the marks on her wrists need not have been caused by suicide attempts, but by violent sexual games. She had come to me without a past, but like the Peermain claimant, she had a backer. Alex needed something from me, and I had already arranged that he get it.

I bent down to the flowers and untwisted the tie from the stems. As I loosened it the cellophane crackled as it had done on the day that Archie Sproat was buried. I pulled the card free.

I did not read it again. I walked to a mesh refuse bin filled with dead flowers, stood over it, and tore the card into pieces. I had done that with Judith's letter, and then been weak and foolish enough to piece it back together. This time I made no mistake. I destroyed the card as surely as I had destroyed the note left by the woman Judith had claimed was her mother.

When I walked away I had made certain that our names were in shreds, beyond recovery, and scattered forever among the dry stems and rotting petals.

In another hour I was back home. I spent the entire journey trying to concentrate on the details of reshaping the mound, but I could make no progress. Bitterness and anger shackled my imagination.

Lillian was reading in the study. Behind her the wall of photographs gleamed like a memorial for a vanished life. I whirled enthusiasm around myself as if it were a disguise.

'Great news,' I said, 'I've worked out an idea for the Peermain commission. Ken's delighted with it.'

Lillian remained seated. She did not even look up from her book. 'Good,' she answered flatly.

Something had happened.

Walkers believe they will not sink into a marsh if they cross it swiftly; eager to reach the far side of Lillian's mood, I began to speak too rapidly.

I told her I had decided to use the mound. Possibly it would even be heightened a little, even though there was nothing to stop me demolishing it if I wanted to. I gabbled out my scheme to dig around the edges, plate the sides with a marble shell, make the result as symmetrical and unblemished as a Moghul tomb.

'Good,' she repeated. There was no pleasure in her voice.

In the pause that followed I had a moment of courage.

'All right,' I demanded, 'what's bothering you?'

'Nothing.'

'I don't think so. Why don't you tell me what's happened?'

'Claire rang. She's booked on a flight in three days. I said we'd pick her up from the airport.'

'But that's good news. It'll be great to have her home.'

'There was another call. Someone called Judith Ford.'

It was what I had most feared. Lillian looked straight at me but kept the book open in her lap. My face seized into a mask of guilt.

'What did she want?'

'She wanted to know if you were home.'

I did not have to consider my options. There was no choice but to be brazen. Confidence was essential; it deflected attack like a shield. I cleared my throat.

'Did you tell her where I was?'

'Why should I?'

'Why not? I don't see what you're getting at, Lillian.'

Despite myself I turned to look at the photographs. I knew as I was doing it that the move was like an admission.

'When I asked if I could take a message she said no,' Lillian continued. 'I don't think she expected me to ask for her name. I thought perhaps she'd invented it on the spur of the moment. I can see from your expression that she didn't. If I were you, I'd ring her back straight away.'

'Really?'

'Well, it must be important if it's so secret.'

I forced myself to turn back and meet Lillian's eyes. Her entire body was tense.

'I get plenty of phone calls from women you've never met,' I said. 'They're all to do with business. Isn't that right?'

She refused to answer, so I did it myself.

'Yes, that's right. From what you tell me, the only distinctive thing about this one is that the caller got flustered. I wouldn't know why; your guess is as good as mine. Whatever the reason, she made you think there was a secret between us. You became suspicious. Not because of evidence, not because of an allegation, but because of a flustered voice. Is that right?'

Still she did not answer.

'For God's sake, Lillian, if you're going to accuse me, at least put down the book while you do it.'

She closed it with slow deliberation. 'All right. *Is* there something going on between you?'

I did my best to give my tolerant but dismissive laugh. 'Of course not.'

'It wouldn't be unusual. Middle-aged men have affairs; they expect it of themselves. I see and hear of it often enough in my line of work. In yours the temptations are even greater – all those followers and students, all that time you spend away from home. She sounded young – in her twenties, I would guess. Is that what she is?'

'I suppose so. Yes, she must be.'

'Don't you think you should tell me about her?'

'There's nothing much to tell.'

Silence hung between us like a blade.

'Jamie, you received an unusual letter a few weeks ago. I never found out who wrote it or what was in it, but as soon as you opened it you were taken ill. Was it from her?'

'I told you. It was an old student of mine wanting a reference. Remember? The sickness was a coincidence. It just happened at the same time. That's all.'

'You tried to convince me it was from a man. Then you hid it away from me. Was it from Judith Ford?'

I sensed that it would be better to make a sacrifice.

'Yes.'

Lillian made a small, winded sound, like a tiny grunt. All her fears were being confirmed.

'Why were you taken ill? Did something happen years ago? Was she more than just a student?'

'No, of course not.'

The seconds dripped like a bleeding wound before she spoke again.

'I don't know if I can believe you. At the time you seemed very ill. I was worried about you. You shared more with this girl than you're admitting. You must have.'

'I don't know what to say, Lillian. You want to believe that we were lovers a long time ago. But we weren't.'

'So you're lovers now? Is that what you're saying?'

'No. You know I don't mean that.'

'Are you sleeping with her?'

'Christ,' I said, and turned to the wall again. Lillian's face, and Claire's, stared out from the photograph taken in Paris. We were smiling, wide-eyed, trapped forever in our happiness by the the incandescence of the flash.

'Jamie, did you bring her here to sleep with her?'

'No.'

'Give me some credit. We've been married for a long time. I can tell when you're lying.'

'The answer is still no.'

'Do you swear it?'

'For God's sake, Lillian.'

Again I forced myself to turn. Her face had not softened.

'You had a visitor when I was away.'

'I—'

'Don't deny it. Our cleaning lady told me you'd had a guest. I told her I didn't think so. She said there must have been, because she had the sheets from one of the guest rooms to wash. The new sheets hadn't been put on the bed very well so she re-did them. You never were much good at housework.'

'When did she tell you this?'

'The morning after I came back.'

'You've been brooding that long?'

'Longer. I asked her where you'd been the previous morning. She told me you were in your workroom and didn't come out. If you hadn't locked yourself up like a hermit then she would have asked you about the sheets. You'd have been able to cover up your little secret. You should have thought of that. You haven't been very good at hiding your tracks, either.'

'And did she tell you that our bed had been slept in as well? She didn't, did she?'

'Even if it had been, it would have made no difference.'

'All right. All right. Judith Ford was here. She slept in a guest room with her boyfriend.'

'Boyfriend,' Lillian repeated dismissively.

I seized the initiative.

'And do you know why she was here? Because she's my assistant on the Peermain project. She has no other income. Artists often don't have any money at the start of their careers. They do things like this. We all do. She wrote to me asking if I could help, and I needed an assistant.'

'You have people who often work with you. They're like a team.'

'And they'll work with me again when the project gets under way. But there's nothing for them to do yet. Everything is still in the planning stage. You know that. Judith Ford helped me with the planning, that's all. She just happened to be the first one to ask.'

'I see. Tell me: do you think it somehow lessens your guilt if you slept with your mistress in one of the guest beds? As for a boyfriend – I don't believe she has one. You've invented him. This woman wants you. She's after you, just you, either for esteem or money, I don't know which. And you've been short-sighted enough to let her work alongside you.'

'You're wrong.'

'Am I? You've never, *never* mentioned her to me. What other conclusion could I reach? I've been suspicious for weeks now. Your personality's changed. You're moody and short-tempered—'

'If things aren't going right with a project I'm often moody and short-tempered. And I looked at your cheque stubs. One is blank. Are you paying your mistress for services rendered?'

'What are you, Lillian? Some kind of private detective?'

'Just a wife trying to find out the truth about her husband.'

'Look, I made a mistake writing out a cheque. I destroyed it and started again. All the right details are on the next stub. That's why the previous one is blank. Check the account if you don't believe me.'

'*I* wrote the next cheque, Jamie.'

I looked at the floor. I did not know what to say. Lillian went on.

'You get a letter which you hide away from me. You issue a cheque without recording any details. You come home with a face scratched by a woman's fingernails and expect me to swallow an unbelievable story about a crazy dog and its even crazier owner. You allow yourself to go weeks overdue on one of the most important commissions you've ever had. You have a secret visitor when I'm away, whom you never tell anyone about. You get a strange phone call from a woman who won't even leave a message. Do you love her?'

The question was like a slap across the face. There was a defined moment in time when it could be refused; too quick a refusal, or too slow, meant that I would not believed.

'Of course not,' I said, but I waited too long before I said it. I felt my life turn as if on an axis.

'I never thought I'd ask you this, Jamie, but I have to know: how serious is it? Think before you answer. If you want our marriage to end, at least be honest with me. Don't sneak away like a coward. You owe me that; we've been together for a long time.'

'Lillian, listen to me.'

'Don't lie.'

My voice shook with emotion. 'I mean what I say. I don't want our marriage to break up. I love you. I've never loved anyone else.'

'Apart from Judith Ford.'

I shook my head. 'It's not like that.'

'What *is* it like, then?'

'More complicated.'

Silence lengthened between us.

Unable to face Lillian, aware that I could not turn again to the display of awards photographs, I looked at the far wall.

There was my desert sand being lowered into ice. When that shot had been taken, not too long ago, my life had been as busy and as cossetted as an opera singer's. All I had seen ahead of me was progress – ever wider recognition, ever richer reward, with an attractive wife who loved and supported me and a talented daughter of whom we were both endlessly proud, and whom we never thought of as adopted. Yet within the last few weeks I had been transformed into a vacillating liar. Today I had been further weakened, compromised, humiliated. The blows that rained upon me were without mercy.

My mind raced but could make no purchase. I sank into hopelessness.

I had done nothing to deserve this. My faults were venial, even amateurish when compared to the sins of others. There had been a good and often noble reason for every action that I had taken. I had done everything in good faith, to secure not only my own life, but also the lives of those I loved.

And now that life was collapsing around me. Like Archie Sproat, I had been slandered and accused. The injustice of it all washed through me in a great swelling wave of self-pity and despair.

I did not even know that I was crying until Lillian crossed the room, took some tissues from a box and pressed them into my hand.

'Wipe your eyes,' she said efficiently, 'I hate to see you like this.'

I needed to be as unjust to someone as life had been to me; she was the easiest target.

'You're the one who caused it,' I said. The sentence came out in a clotted snarl.

'I don't think so, Jamie. I think you've brought it all on yourself.'

I lowered my head so that I was staring at the floor. This

made the tears worse. My vision swam, salt sharpened in my mouth, and quite abruptly I became aware that thick, slimy mucus was running from my nose.

A tiny, still part of me stood aside and sneered that I was both pitiful and absurd.

The tissues were bunched in my fist. Lillian took my hand, opened it, extracted them and put one to my eyes to wipe them. I jerked away my head like a truculent child but she repeated the action. This time I let her do it.

'Come on,' she said. 'I know you've been foolish, Jamie. It's been written all over you for weeks. Maybe no one else could see it, but I know you better than anyone else.'

I took a lungful of air and made a shuddering, animal-like noise that distressed me even more.

'I think you should stop this,' she went on. 'It's not doing you any good. Isn't that right?'

I moved my head, but did not even know if I was agreeing with her.

'At least try,' she insisted.

'I've got myself in too deep,' I confessed. The words felt as if they had been gummed together.

'Yes, you have. The important thing now is to get out of it.'

'I never want to see her again, Lillian.'

'Right.'

'I've been stupid and good-hearted and all she does is prey on me.'

'I'm not surprised. These girls know what they're doing. Men of your age are so vain and foolish. If you're well-known and rich, then you're a prime target. What did she do – beg you to help her?'

I nodded.

'And before you knew it, you'd fallen for the oldest lines in the business.'

I put my hands to my eyes and wiped away the tears

that still welled from them. They were hot against my fingers.

'Something like that,' I sniffled.

'It's best if you rid yourself of her, Jamie.'

'I know.'

'Cut her out of your life completely. Ring back and order her not to bother you ever again. Then we can both forget her. She's not worth remembering.'

Lillian moved closer to me and embraced me soothingly.

'We'll survive,' she said. 'We'll always have each other.'

I was comforted and reassured, but I did not want to be denied my moment of victory and revenge.

'I have to see her. Just once.'

The tension lessened in Lillian's embrace; I could feel it transfer to her body.

'There's something Judith Ford has to do,' I explained weakly. 'It's already been planned. It won't take more than a couple of hours. Then I'll tell her that it's all over. I promise.'

'What's been planned? Someone else will have to do it.'

'They could, but it would put back the project by a fortnight. Three weeks, maybe. I can't afford to let that happen. You know how late I am already.'

Lillian did not say anything.

'I want rid of this woman even more than you do,' I insisted. 'You're right; I've been stupid and naïve and it's unfair on you, unfair on all we've shared. She's nothing to me. I swear it.'

There was a longer pause. It seemed that the ground tilted beneath my feet.

'You can trust me,' I said, 'I'm not a liar.'

'Then you'd better ring her back,' Lillian said carefully.

'All right. I'll do it later.'

'No. Do it now.'

I waited for her to go on.

'I want this finished, Jamie. I don't want it to linger. Do what you have to do, and then end it.'

I rang Judith from the workroom, all the while waiting to hear if Lillian picked up the extension to eavesdrop. It was what I would have done in her position, but I heard no tell-tale click.

'Judith?'

'It's you,' she said. 'My God, I'm sorry. I thought your wife was away.'

'You picked the wrong day. What do you want?'

'Are you all right? I'm sorry if I caused a problem; it was unthinking of me. When your wife answered I panicked and made things worse. It's just that I got so excited at Alex's news that I felt I had to tell you.'

'What news?'

'A man from a gallery I've never heard of made an appointment to see him. He came round this morning. He said he was looking for artists called new traditionalists. He liked some of Alex's work; he's even talking about placing a dozen in an exhibition. It wouldn't just be Alex, there would be other painters as well, but it's still wonderful news. Don't you think so? He's getting on the ladder at last.'

'I'm pleased.'

There was a fractional pause. 'Do you know about this?'

'The Tetmajer, was it?'

'That's right.'

'Alex would have been selected on his own merits. But listen to me; I can't talk long. I need an assistant – just for a few hours. It's nothing difficult. I need some trees marked out for felling. I'd like you to do it.'

'Alex and me?'

'Alex has enough to think about with his exhibition. No, just you. Tomorrow. Will you do it?'

'Is this at the estate?'

'Yes, but we'll not be visiting the house. I'll pick you up

and drive you there, but you may have to come back by train. I'll get you a ticket, if it comes to that. And I'll pay you the official hourly rate for the work. Will you do it?'

'You know I want to visit the site.'

'Right,' I said, 'we're agreed.'

I arranged a time, confirmed that I would pick her up, and then said goodbye.

I was surprised, chilled, impressed by my own efficiency. I had not acted like that for a long, long time. Judith would have thought that I was ending the call because Lillian was in earshot. I had given away nothing. She probably had no suspicions at all.

I went back downstairs and held out my hand. Lillian grasped it and looked at me.

'In twenty-four hours we'll both be able to forget her,' I said.

6

I planned to confront Judith before we even left the city. I pictured her, numbed and humiliated by my discovery of the truth, tearfully begging my forgiveness. She would confess that the entire plan had been drawn up by Alex. I would appear to relent a little, drive her to the estate, and take her to the wood. There I would turn on her like the most surgical of advocates and itemise her duplicity and her failings with a cold, unrelenting zeal.

But Judith was so girlishly enthusiastic about our journey, so thankful, so adamant that she was privileged, that I delayed the crisis until later. Even the clothes she wore – her torn jeans and an old white blouse – seemed youthful and naïve enough to deflect accusations of malice.

As I drove she asked question after question about my design for the mound. Soon I was talking about it in detail, like a soldier confessing to an enemy.

As we neared the estate I thought of taking the road to the cemetery. I could take Judith to the Sproat grave, tell their sad story, study her reaction. Archie Sproat, too, had been a helpless victim of lies; perhaps sympathy and conscience would make her confess. But I rejected the notion. Whenever I had visited the grave I had felt too vulnerable. It was not the place for either confrontation or judgement.

We arrived at the estate, were checked at the gate, and then followed the long drive. I parked beside the house and took a large spool of marker tape from the boot. A peacock, watching us from the crest of the nearest Interlocking Piece, raised its tail in a rustling, shimmering fan.

As we walked across the parkland Judith did not limp at all.

The wood was in full leaf now, and the narrow path was overgrown. Flowers starred the grass and tight blossoms hung on the rhododrendrons. The air was humid with growth. I stuck my knife into the bark of the first trunk to be selected.

'We'll start here,' I said.

Judith placed her bag on the ground and rolled up her sleeves.

The line was chosen with an architect's care. We followed it at shoulder height, systematically moving from tree to tree, lashing the white marker tape as tightly as a garrotte around each trunk. Time passed quickly. Judith was a good assistant, and the rhythm of our task meant that we concentrated on that and that alone. We talked little, and then only about the demarcation. After a short while I even stopped thinking about the moment that must come. Sometimes, however, I imagined Eve conscientiously taping all the gaps through which the rooms might breathe.

It took us more than an hour to reach the last and first tree. My knife was still protruding from the bark. A sudden breeze stirred the leaf canopy and made patches of brightness shiver along the trunks.

The wood's division was a signal, I thought; a silent announcement that the future was taking shape. I placed the almost-empty spool next to Judith's bag. A few yards of unused tape hung like fuse cable between the spool and the tree. I looped it in my hand like a lasso and pulled the knife out of the trunk.

'It looks as if we're finished,' Judith said. There was pride in her voice, as if she herself had planned the work.

'That's right,' I said, not looking at her as I made the cut. Severed tape fell to either side. I felt not excitement but a strange emptiness. I closed the knife and placed it on top of the spool.

Judith put her hands into her hair and pushed it away from her face. Her fingers were grimy with bark and soil. 'Are you satisfied?' she asked.

'I believe so.'

The marker tape was strung as taut as any tightrope. I raised my hand to touch it. The white line quivered. I imagined soldiers, their sight clouded by mustard gas, following a ribbon leading them back to safety. If such a casualty were to follow our guide he would not even realise that he had been led back to where he had started.

Judith was looking from side to side, following the line. 'This place is odd,' she said. 'I started to think so a while ago. It gives me a feeling I've never had before.'

Suddenly conscious that I might seem neurotic I released the tape. White surfaces flashed against the greenery like drawn blades.

'The completed sculpture will be here for centuries,' I said. 'Some people find that difficult to accept. We've formed a habit of thinking in terms of the immediate.'

'It's not that. I've already got used to a kind of immortality.'

'I don't understand.'

'In a couple of months' time hundreds, maybe thousands of people will examine every detail of Alex's studies of me. Those images won't die. They won't be destroyed or forgotten or left to rot. They'll still be around in the future that you're talking about.'

It was a vain and foolish illusion. I did not dispute it.

'There's a difference here,' she went on.

'It's because you know that nothing about the sculpture can be changed. A drawing or a painting can be altered even when it's at an advanced stage. But there's no margin of error in sculpture or architecture. Permanence is a condition of the work. My kind of art is no different to an exact science.'

I looked down through the trees towards the parkland. I could glimpse it through the undergrowth of shrub and rhododendron.

'We've done what we can, Judith. I don't need you any more.'

It was as if I had not spoken. She picked up her bag and slung it over her shoulder. 'It's something about your blueprint for the site. Something familiar.'

'Come on,' I said, taking a few steps down the slope, 'it might be as well if we left here for a short while.'

'Are you leaving the spool?'

'I'll come back for it.'

'Are you going to introduce me to your friends in the house?'

'Not a chance. I told you we wouldn't go there.'

'You could say I was your paid assistant. That's right, isn't it? You're employing me.'

'Yes, you helped, and you'll be paid. But I didn't really need help. And I don't want my sponsors to meet you. After all, they may see a family likeness.'

I pitched the last sentence to be as sour as possible, but Judith did not react. Instead she studied me carefully as I took a few more steps. I knew that she was comparing my face to her own.

'I don't think so,' she said at last. 'The resemblance isn't striking.'

'No? Don't you think there's *some* likeness?'

'Similarity isn't the point.'

I found the path and followed it down towards the edge of

the wood. As the thicket cleared I could see the Interlocking Piece in front of me, lying on its side like a felled totem only half-carved.

'After all,' Judith continued, and I wondered if I could detect a disguised worry in her voice, 'not every daughter resembles her father. Or her mother.'

'When we first met I imagined that you looked like Eve. Later I thought you looked a little like me. Now I know that I was wrong.'

'You've changed your mind?'

'Yes.'

We reached the edge of the wood. I strode across the grass until I reached the sculpture. Then I folded my arms, leaned against it, and turned to face Judith. I had already postponed the moment of truth too often. Now I knew there could be little further delay.

Judith followed me to the Interlocking Piece and stood at the far end with her hands spread on its surface like a faith-healer's.

I gathered my courage. 'Listen to me,' I said.

She took no notice, but moved her fingers across the grain as if she were a blind person seeking meaning within its texture. 'Your book says this is in seven parts,' she said.

'It is.'

'It says that they slot together to make a shape like a star.'

'That's right.'

'Except that you would need cranes to fit them into each other. You've said as much yourself.'

'So?'

'Do they really lock together?'

I said nothing. The breeze stirred her hair.

'Oh, I know they look as if they do, but I doubt it. Someone like you would think it clever if secretly they didn't. Maybe a few parts connect, but not all of them.'

I shook my head. She paused, and then gave the wide grin of success.

'I know what it is. There's a missing piece.'

I did not answer.

'Am I right? They all fit together, partly, but there's a key that should lock them in place – and you never made that. That's right, isn't it? It's a game. You once told me you played with your audience. Now I understand why. Because your audience thinks that puzzles and abstraction and misplacement and paradox are the same thing as insight.'

I looked down.

'I'm a good critic, aren't I?' she asked, her voice saturated with self-congratulation. 'Eventually someone will plot the shapes on a computer and discover that they don't really interlock; they fall apart. There will be academic arguments about why you did what you did, and what the true meaning must be. Do you dream that this won't happen until after your death? Some dead artists are still controversial. You'd like to be one of them. These pieces are part of your gamble for immortality.'

'You think so?'

'You give yourself away, Jamie. You *do*. Your work tells people more about yourself than you realise. Even the tree-trunk in the gallery suggested something – not just to me, but to that other woman as well. When you walked out I turned back to ask why she was so intrigued by your piece. Perhaps she was bored by her husband's knowingness, perhaps she thought I was a kindred spirit; I don't know. But she held onto my arm like a sister.'

'Or a mother?'

'What?'

'It doesn't matter. Go on.'

'She told me that it suggested fertility.'

'Why? Because it was a tree?'

'Of course not. Brancusi made egg-shaped pieces of bronze into things that most people recognise as heads. You selected a bulbous trunk that some of us recognise as a pregnant woman. Of course, I expect you to deny it.'

'That's right,' I said firmly, 'I deny it. The trouble with abstract art is that undeveloped minds read their own fantasies into it.'

Anger shone momentarily in her eyes. I wondered if she might attack me again.

'You're protecting yourself. I understand why. You want your sculpture to be seen as difficult. Alex says you want to be arcane and cerebral.'

'He looked up those words, did he?'

'But your work isn't just for mandarins, is it? Not just for the élite? Anyone who has looked closely knows that it's about women and men and birth and death.'

'This is ridiculous. Try to be a little more mature. Art isn't so mechanical. Neither is life.'

'I don't think it's mechanical. I think it's symbolic.'

'That's because you're convinced that art holds meaning like a fruit holds seed. Open it up, and there's what you want. Alex believes that. It's simple and it's reductionist, but his arguments have convinced you because you don't know any better. Let's be honest; his portraits are easy. Their appearance is what they are; that's their appeal and their limitation. Their principal demand on the viewer is identification. He could have been working back in the time of Gainsborough. My work operates on a much more complex level.'

'Which can be opened up almost as easily. Come on, Jamie – what are your most successful pieces? Slots in the ground? A needle pointing at the sky? Sand in ice? A bulbous tree? What inspired pieces like that?'

'I never use the word *inspiration*.'

'All right, what gave them their shape? You're not analytic and you're not objective. Your life is in those pieces.

You're just like Alex; forever mining your experiences and your obsessions. One day they'll be exhausted.'

'I thought you were merely ignorant. Now I see that you're neurotic. You're the second person in two days to force absurd interpretations onto me. You couldn't be more wrong. My work is completely removed from my own life. To suggest otherwise is wishful thinking. But I know your motives.'

'Who else said it?'

'It doesn't matter. He didn't go as far as you.'

A peacock's harsh, resonant cry filled the air for several seconds. Judith would not be halted.

'Who was it?'

'A man who arranges my sponsorship. He thinks the finished mound will resemble an eye.'

There was a moment's pause. I could hear the leaf canopy rustle.

'An eye?' she repeated.

'And you're crazy enough to agree.'

'I don't see it as an eye.'

'I'm surprised.'

'The way you described it, it will be more like a birth.'

I felt the earth turn on its axis.

Judith spoke to me from a cloud. I could not hear what she said, and I had no idea how much time had passed. It might have been only a few seconds, but it could have been minutes. During that immeasurable moment my imagination was hundreds of feet high, freed from gravity, and I looked down to see the head of the mound force its unstoppable way out of land that gaped in furrows around it.

'You planned this,' I whispered.

'I don't understand.'

I breathed deeply several times before I spoke again. She looked at me with a concern I knew to be false.

'Don't lie,' I said. 'You knew that I was onto you. That's why you're trying to tie my life to my art. You conjure up symbols that don't exist, just to make me doubt the truth.'

'I've been honest about what I think. I'm sorry that you've taken offence.'

Now a slow rage gripped and consumed me. I was furious at my own gullibility.

'I know all about you, Judith.'

'Of course you don't. There's always more to tell.'

'You admit it?'

'What are you talking about, Jamie? You *don't* know all about me. You usually act as if you don't *want* to know. In fact you prefer to find out from Alex, rather than ask me. Why do you do that? Don't you trust me?'

'I don't trust either of you. You're both in it together. But I think he must have started it.'

Her face deepened.

'Started what? For God's sake, we're having a disagreement about sculpture. You got used to such arguments before I was born. You even told me once that you didn't care if you were misunderstood. But now everything seems to have changed.'

'That's right. It's changed.'

She shook her head in exasperation, opened her bag and put one hand in it.

'There's nothing in there to help,' I said.

'I once gave you a mirror to see yourself in. You should see your face now.'

'Alex had access to art college libraries, didn't he?'

She pulled the mirror from her bag, snapped it open, and held it out to me. I refused to look.

'Didn't he?'

She thrust the mirror towards me. It was the same one she had used behind the gallery, and out of the corner of my eye I saw that hatred had inhabited the reflection of my face. I lashed out with my arm, caught Judith on the wrist, and sent the mirror flying. It fell nearby, its two silvered surfaces reflecting the sky so that circles of blue shone up from the grass.

'That hurt,' she said, nursing her wrist. 'Are you trying to pay me back? I thought we'd gone beyond that.'

'When did he see the article?'

'I told you. Just before I wrote—'

'Not that one. The one that was written just after you were born.'

'I don't know anything about that. You never told me about it. Was I mentioned? And Eve?'

'Stop acting, Judith. I assume that's your real name. One thing's certain, it was never Grace.'

She turned pale within an instant. The flush disappeared from her cheeks as if in an illusion, and for a moment I thought she would fall to the ground in a faint. Even her eyes seemed to dim.

I was triumphant. At last I was in control. I had seized the moment; it was mine. Judith Ford and Alex Sylianou no longer had power over me.

'There's one thing I don't know,' I said. My speech was steadier now. 'I don't know if you ever knew Grace McGoldrick. You can at least tell me that.'

Judith's lips moved, but her voice was so tiny I could not hear it.

'What?'

'I'm Grace McGoldrick.' The name faded into silence as she tried to speak it.

I was unforgiving. 'I think it's possible that you're someone called Judith Ford. You've never been my daughter. You're someone who saw the main chance and took it. For a while I believed in you, but now I've come to my senses. You're nothing to do with me. You're as alien and as mercenary as the Peermain claimant, and I was taken in as easily as some of that family.'

'I don't understand. Who's the Peermain claimant?'

'Anna Anderson? You've heard of her? She was nothing to do with the Tsar's daughter. But you're no Anna Anderson. She hoodwinked the public for years. You've already been found out.'

'I've never heard of her, either,' Judith said. Her tones were strengthening and colour was returning to her cheeks. 'Who are these people? What have they got to do with me?'

'Confidence tricksters. Charlatans who impersonated missing heirs. Fellow criminals.'

'You don't believe I'm Grace? How can you be blind to the obvious?'

'Where's the proof? Come on – where is it?'

'Do you think I'm just after your money? Is that it?'

'What else would be behind it?'

'Jamie, you're my father. I know you've never been happy with the truth, but it can't be altered. Neither of us can forget what we've learned. As for money, if I'd wanted it that badly, I'd have cashed your cheque, not destroyed it.'

'I grant you that was a clever move. Professional enough to fool me for a while. It's always best to pretend that you're indifferent to what you crave. Who are you? Did the Fords adopt Grace as your sister? Is that it? What happened to my real daughter? Does she know nothing about me? Maybe she's dead by now, or in an asylum, or just working quietly somewhere, unaware that you've stolen her name. Where is she, Judith?'

Judith turned to the Interlocking Piece and spread her hands across it. Her fingers were extended so that I could see them tremble.

Her answer was like a statement to a judge. 'There was

only me, no one else. The Fords adopted me because they couldn't have children of their own.'

I thought of Claire, who had come to us before she could talk, and who was far away on the other side of the Atlantic, her life growing apart from both Lillian's and my own.

'I didn't believe them when they told me the truth,' Judith continued. 'I'd gone through that fantasising, worrying time that all pubescent girls have – the time when you become convinced that something happened that you can't remember, and that your parents aren't your real parents, and that you're not a genuine member of the family at all, but a kind of foundling. I'd gone through it and come out of the other side. And I'd been right all along. The night I was told was the worst night of my life.'

'You can stop the invention, Judith. The game's over. You lost.'

'The Fords couldn't control me any more, so I thought they were taking revenge. In a way they were; truth was their revenge. That was when I was handed the birth certificate. It was like a warrant. I wanted to tear it up but I couldn't. Just like you wanted to tear up my letter. Just like I tore up your cheque. But I kept it. I can show it to you.'

'Copies of birth certificates are easy to get. You just have to pretend to be the person named on it. And I didn't want my daughter ever to know who her real parents were.' I halted, chilled by another thought. 'You might have known her. You might know who she really is.'

'*I*'m your daughter. I'd be lying if I denied it.'

'You swear you don't know her?'

'I can't tell you any more clearly. I'm Grace. Grace is me. We're the same person.'

'Listen. A long time ago, just after Grace was born, I was interviewed for a magazine called *Art And Artists*. Right?'

Judith shook her head helplessly. 'I don't know. How would I know that?'

'Eve died before the issue was printed. There wasn't much about me – just a black-and-white reproduction of an early work and mention of my wife and daughter. I called myself Mick in those days, but the reporter asked me my full name and printed it. That article is the only document from my early life that I haven't been able to completely destroy.'

'So my name's mentioned? And Mother's?'

'Grace's and Eve's are, yes. But Grace and Eve have both vanished forever. And so has the man I used to be.'

Judith moved her head away sharply, like someone pulling away from a blow.

'If I visit a new gallery or college I ask to spend time in the archives. There's never a problem with access; I'm too well-known and respected. They automatically trust me. But if I can find that magazine from a quarter of a century ago I take it from its file, smuggle it out and destroy it.'

I paused. She stared at me from a drawn, frightened face. I went on.

'But I've not been able to destroy every one. Alex must have found a copy. Did he stumble on it by chance, Judith? Or did he go searching for my surname through the indexes?'

'He hasn't seen it. Neither of us has. We didn't even know it existed.'

'After reading that article it would be easy. The clues were all there; a search in the Public Records Office would confirm what you wanted to know.'

'You're making all this up. It's lunatic. You don't realise how wrong you are.'

'Then you took your big chance. You gambled that Eve and Grace were no longer part of my life, that they'd either fled or died. Not too much of a gamble, when you consider it. No other profile of me has ever mentioned them. It couldn't. Your risks were slight compared to the ones taken by the Peermain claimant. What would you have done if I'd reported you to the police? Denied everything? But the letter was in your handwriting—'

I stopped. How could I be certain that the letter was in her handwriting? I had seen no other examples.

'Or did you get someone to write it for you? One of your friends from the squat, willing to do anything for a few pounds? That way, if things had gone wrong from the start, you could have claimed the letter was malicious. You could say it was nothing to do with you.'

Her face had the blank, uncomprehending look of a disaster victim. I knew she was unable to answer me. From far away, like a lazy tide creeping onto a deserted shore, I felt a distant flow of sadness. But I was determined not to be stopped.

'After that everything must have fallen into place. All you had to do was assume a stranger's name and watch. I implicated myself minute by minute. There were signposts for you all along the way. Alex was even there when someone called me Mick. I pretended I didn't know her.'

'How can you believe that everything was so planned? An impostor would never argue, never insult you. And certainly never hit you. She wouldn't jeopardise her chances. Can't you see that?'

'I can see that you're clever enough not to make things too easy. You once told me you'd been an actress. I didn't realise how good you were.'

Breath hissed through her teeth.

'Your whole operation was complicated and subtle,' I went on. 'You must have thought success was just within your grasp. What were you going to do? Start bleeding me slowly, like expert torturers? Did you hope that by the time I realised the truth I'd be so weak that

I could do nothing about it? Would you have threatened to expose me to Lillian by then? You must have wanted me to be as helpless and pathetic as a blackmail victim.'

'I don't want to destroy your marriage. Neither does Alex. Why should we?'

'Then why did you telephone my house and speak to Lillian? Was that a warning? Had you spent too long a time without my money? Did you think I would be so compromised I would begin paying you out straight away?'

'You know why I rang. I shouldn't have done. I'm sorry. But you got yourself out of it.'

I did not answer.

'You got yourself out?' This time it was a question.

'I told Lillian you were an old student looking for a job for your boyfriend. She didn't fully believe me.'

There was a pause, a fracture. I confessed.

'She thinks we're lovers,' I said.

The breeze grew stronger, harrying the grass into rippling crescents. As it passed across us it stirred our clothes and tangled Judith's hair. I heard it shake the leaves in the copse before it died away.

'You denied it,' she said.

'I tried to.'

'I thought you and Lillian both trusted each other?'

'We do.'

Realisation broke across her.

'My God, Jamie, you confessed. You confessed to something you didn't do.'

'It was easier than the truth.'

Judith made one hand into a small, tight fist and hit the side of the sculpture. A dull, dead sound came from the wood. She raised her hand and hit again, but harder this time. I thought I heard her knuckles crack. When she lifted her fist away I could see that it was already swollen and discoloured.

'You'll do anything to protect yourself,' she said. 'I should have known you hadn't changed.'

We stood together, separated by lies, while the world went on all around us. I became aware that I could hear a bee as it buzzed among the plants at the edge of the wood; that there were cars driving along the unseen road past the church; that the smell of a rich summer rose from the land. Suddenly, without reason, I thought of my cube of compacted sand moving ever more swiftly to the decaying snout of the glacier.

Judith turned and walked back into the wood.

I heard the sound of her footsteps change, from the mossy sighs of the parkland to the smothering rasp of longer grass, and then there was a dark, marshy sound as her weight compressed a patch of last year's fallen leaves. I watched as illumination faded around her and the weak dappling sunlight grew fainter on her shoulders. Ahead of her the white tape sliced the greenery and shadow like a horizontal razor-cut across an ancient canvas.

I stood by the Interlocking Piece for some time, running one hand across its surface.

The texture was changing. Five years ago I had been as precise as a strategist in selecting the distribution pattern of the individual pieces. On that day the seasoned wood was still unweathered, and each section resembled a huge, expensive ornament about to be sanded and waxed. Even the faces I had left rough-hewn seemed as if at any moment they would be planed to a final perfection. Now sun, rain, and frost had insinuated their way into the grain. Widening splits could be seen in the wood and tiny insects had bored holes into it. At the outer edges, where the trunk lay exposed in cross-section, deeper fissures had opened. There was a hidden face near the underside. I bent to run my fingers across it; they came away blotched with damp fungal spores the colour of gangrene.

I knelt down and wiped my fingers on the grass. Circles of sky still shone from the open mirrors. I looked up into the copse. Judith had vanished. I had thought she might snap the ribbon, but it was still taut between the trees, like an unbroken finishing tape.

I stood up, rubbed my hands together, and shouted her name. Its resonance died within the foliage.

'I know you can hear me,' I called after a few seconds. There was still no answer.

I walked to the edge of the wood as a gust tossed the branches along its flank. One of the thin, high trunks swayed with a noise like a mewling kitten.

'It's time for us to go,' I shouted. 'I can't leave you here.'

I thought I heard a response, but then decided I had imagined it. I stepped back into the wood.

Within a few feet I caught my ankle in a loop of thorn. Kicking would not shake it free so I bent and gingerly removed the shoot. As I did so the barbs pricked my hand. Droplets of blood squeezed up out of the tiny punctures.

I put my hand to my mouth and licked it. When I looked again the texture of my palm had become more clearly defined. Blood gathered on it in smudged blooms. I licked the skin again, wiped my hand on the side of my trousers, and set off walking towards the centre of the wood.

There was still no sign of Judith. The spool lay on the ground and the severed end of the tape hung loosely from the trunk of the first and last tree. But there was no knife. I looked around the spool and kicked at a nearby patch of fern, but I knew that the knife had not fallen there. Judith had taken it.

I ducked under the tape and immediately stumbled across an unseen bough, fallen years ago and now half-buried in a mulch of decaying leaves. When I looked back I saw the marks of my own shoes imprinted in the dark mass like moulds waiting to be filled. All the time I drew nearer and nearer to the centre of the wood.

When I reached the edge of the mound I thought Judith must be on the other side. I imagined her, sullen and judged, seated with her back to the incline, as isolated and protected from me as possible. But when I walked around the perimeter she was still nowhere to be seen.

'Judith?' I asked the silence.

I looked into the far side of the copse and up onto the flanks of the mound. Only after several seconds did I notice indentations in the mossy grass and a sapling branch that was broken but not severed. The exposed wood was pale as new ivory. I put my hand around the main stem and tugged; it easily took my weight.

'I'm coming up,' I shouted. I did not expect an answer, but I waited for one before I began to climb.

Near the summit the back of Judith's head came into view. She was standing on the edge of the mound, at the far side of the shallow depression, looking away from me and out across the treetops towards the roof of the Peermain house.

As soon as I reached the top of the mound I stood still. Judith knew I was there, but she remained staring outwards with her arms folded. Between us scores of dandelions and daisies swivelled and nodded in the wind.

'I've been calling for you,' I said.

The wind stirred our hair and clothes, and all around the mound the leaf canopy billowed gently.

'Are you going to answer me?'

'You reject me and then you want me,' she said without turning. 'I'm tired of it.'

'Just admit that you lied.'

She said nothing. I licked my hand again.

'Tell me the truth. That's all I want.'

'You want me to help you to forget me? You think that an admission will wash away my memory?'

'I want your confession. That's all.'

'I'll not give you that satisfaction. You're going to remember me for a long time. You'll never be able to stop thinking of me. Every time you see someone who looks a little like me. Every time someone talks about the work you did here. Every time you ransack an archive. I'll take over your mind. When you think of Claire you'll think of me. On the day you die you'll still remember.'

I drew in a deep breath; there was a shudder in my throat.

'I didn't want much,' she said, 'just the simple things. The things you're so keen to protect.'

I licked my hand again.

'But I've been betrayed by everyone,' she went on, 'even by my own mother and father.'

'You're not persuading me, Judith. Those days are over. You may as well give up.'

We stood without speaking for what seemed like a long time. The wind buffeted us.

'You can't stay here,' I insisted.

She turned. The knife was in her right hand.

Fear shook me as strongly as the wind. Normally Judith would be easy to overpower, but this was not normal. She had already marked me once; this time a betrayed, insane rage could make her unbeatable. A few seconds would be all that was needed for a fatal cut. Alone, unheeded, I could bleed to death on this mound. I had often dreamed of sinking with a ship. Now it seemed that I was a man adrift on high, floating wreckage, with the sea of leaves washing all around me, and that I could die here, murdered by the only other survivor.

'Let's be careful,' I heard myself say weakly. I glanced behind to see if I could step back any further without falling. I could not.

Judith held the knife higher. Liquid sunlight ran across the steel.

'Careful to be accurate, you mean? Don't worry, I've had some practice.'

She was holding the knife in the wrong position for an attack. A cut through the air would be badly angled, even ineffectual. Suddenly I realised that the danger she threatened was not to me, but to herself.

My mind and senses were flooded by a giddy, timeless jubilation. Just as it had done when I had discovered Eve's body, a limitless euphoria invaded me as sharply as an injection straight into the bloodstream. Everything blazed with its own potential, and for a few moments I breathed free, rich, endless air.

And then realities crashed around me like prison doors being slammed. I could never explain Judith's suicide, or our relationship, either to Lillian or to the police. My marriage would be broken forever by such an act. Even my livelihood and freedom could be threatened.

I wanted to say something so honest and true that it would make Judith throw the knife aside, but I could think of nothing.

'You don't think I'll do it?' she asked. 'Didn't Alex tell you about my history of instability? Wasn't it part of your man-to-man talk? And haven't you told me how my mother was just like me? Weren't you expecting me to do something like this?'

'No. Of course not.'

'Alex told you everything, didn't he?'

'He said he'd rescued you.'

But I had come to doubt what Alex had told me. I had even decided that there was a different reason for the marks on Judith's wrists.

She was acting.

To stand in front of me and threaten suicide was a desperate ploy, a melodramatic ruse to shame me into believing her. She did not realise the sudden breadth of my confidence, or that I would never submit. She was like a jackal who had feasted too long on the marrow of my credulity; I was ready for revenge.

'I don't know if you're like your mother,' I said with a new, heartless confidence. 'I don't know who your real mother was.'

'Leave me alone.'

'It's too late to beg.'

'Let me get this over with. It won't take long. You can discover me just like you discovered Eve.'

I was still convinced Judith would do nothing.

'No last messages?' I sneered. 'No confessions?'

'None. Go.'

'Pretending you're going to copy Eve doesn't alter the truth. Neither do histrionics. I know the difference between falsehood and reality. We're nothing to each other. We never have been.'

Judith extended her left arm towards me, the fist half-closed. The grimy fingers were curled upwards like a flower contracted on itself. I saw the scars quite clearly. They were as pale as animal tracks across tidal sand.

'You're wrong,' she said. 'I'll prove it.'

Her voice was quietly resolute. She raised the knife high above her other wrist. Sunlight tempered the blade and made it merciless as a guillotine.

It was Judith's measured calm that made me lunge forward.

As I reached for the knife her eyes shone with feral excitement. A detached part of myself scoffed at my participation in such a scene. Judith had no intention of harming herself. Her posture was studied. She was more like a priestess in a lurid Hollywood drama than someone determined to sever her own artery. Once I took hold of the raised wrist and twisted hard, the knife would tumble from her grip. I was certain of that.

I almost missed. Her hand began its downward swing as I grasped it. Tension bunched in her forearm. She did not give up, but continued to force the knife down towards her other wrist.

Her determination and strength threw me off-balance. I tried to find a firm foothold in the irregular surface of the depression and brought up my other arm. My elbow hit her in the face. I was not sure if this was accidental. I heard bone jar against bone. The electricity of the impact thrilled my arm.

Judith gave a short, breathless grunt. She, too, lost her footing.

For a few seconds we scrambled around each other like duellists struggling for the final blow. The knife shivered and swung like a vane, light sweeping back and forth across the metal.

Quite suddenly it ended. Judith's fist was empty, her hand locked half-open in spasm. The knife lay between us on the vivid green moss. I put my foot on its handle and pressed down hard. It sank fractionally into the soil.

We were locked together in a lovers' cumbersome embrace. I could smell sweat, hers and mine, and feel the thump of both our hearts.

Madly, crazily, I thought of rape.

'Let go,' she said. Dark hair covered her face like a broken screen.

I did not move. I did not want to, did not dare.

'You've won. Let go.'

I released her wrist and heard the faint sound of skin unsticking from skin. Energy drained out of her immediately. Before I could hold on she fell onto her knees at my feet.

Suspicious that she would try to recover the knife, I pressed down even harder. The handle clicked as it lodged against gravel.

Judith did not move. She was as motionless as a discarded puppet, legs doubled up underneath her, head hanging down from stooped shoulders, wrists crossed with their palms upwards. I could see down the front of her shirt and the rip in her jeans had widened further. Her posture gave a turn to the rack of my excited unease.

When I bent to retrieve the knife she still did not react. The only thing that moved was her hair, lifting and tangling in the wind. She could have been a captured rebel dragged before an emperor for sentencing.

'Get up,' I said, stepping back to the far side of the depression. I closed the knife and slipped it into my pocket.

She did not answer, did not move.

'Get up,' I repeated, but roughly this time.

Still no reaction.

I looked around at the shivering foliage. This woman was determined to destroy me, I thought. Even in defeat she was implacable. If everything ended here she would have achieved an aim. I imagined the mound sinking beneath the trees like a volcanic island sliding beneath waves, carrying both our futures down into a green airless darkness within which I would gasp helplessly, just as I had done long ago in a room flooded with gas.

I strode back across the depression, seized Judith by the upper arm, and dragged her to her feet. She neither helped nor resisted me.

'Listen,' I said. 'You've done enough harm. Learn when to stop.'

She looked up with round, widened eyes. I expected to see fear or hatred; instead there was a blankness, as if shock had shut down every emotion as efficiently as someone closing valves.

'I'm taking you back,' I told her.

She did not answer.

'Listen to me. I'm taking you back to my car. Right? Then I'm going to drive you to the nearest railway station and put you on a train. All right?'

There was still no response, and nothing in her eyes.

'For Christ's sake,' I said, exasperated beyond measure, 'try to make it easier for yourself as well as for me. Now come on.'

She was difficult to lead off the mound because the sides were so steep. Halfway down its flank her feet slipped and my grip on her arm was broken. She half-slid, half-rolled to the bottom of the incline.

I slithered down beside her. When I asked if she was hurt she did not answer. Her face was as blank as she could make it, but the shirt gaped open like an invitation. I took hold of its edges and managed to push the buttons back through the holes. My hands were trembling wildly.

The path was too narrow for us to walk side by side, so I had to push her down its slope. We stumbled several times. At one point I lost my footing and fell to the ground. Like a patient animal, Judith waited without emotion while I picked myself up and then took hold of her arm again.

Now I manhandled her across the parkland. We were both limping. A peacock strutted in front of us with magisterial assurance as we reached the car.

I put Judith into the passenger seat. She did not try to fasten the seat belt so I did it for her. As I drove away a bee, heavy with pollen, hit the windscreen and left a powdery smudge of bright gold on the glass.

As soon as we were outside the gates I felt nothing but increased rage and hatred for Judith. I began cursing her with a relentless barrage of invective. I dragged swear-words from my memory and repeated them time after time as if their force were somehow cumulative. In return she sat without a tremor, emotionless as a paralysis victim, gazing ahead unseeingly. It took us twenty minutes to reach the railway station.

It was a small station and there were only a few passengers waiting on the platform. The train was due in ten minutes. I paid the fare to a clerk whose suspicious gaze lingered on both of us. When Judith would not accept the ticket I shoved it into her shirt pocket. I also took all the notes but one from my wallet, folded them, and placed them in the matching pocket. For an artist's assistant it was the equivalent of about two weeks' work.

While she stood on the platform I went to one of the phone booths and dialled Alex. All the time I watched Judith. Her fingers were still grubby, and now her jeans and shirt were marked with grass and soil. Her one exposed knee had been grazed by her slide down the side of the mound. For a brief, fleeting moment I was sorry for her. I brought up my hand to my face and licked it again.

'I'm putting Judith on a train,' I told Alex. 'It leaves in a few minutes. If I were you I'd pick her up at the main station.'

'Is she ill?'

'She's pretending to be shocked. There's nothing really wrong. I found out and confronted her. That's what happened.'

'Found out? What do you mean?'

'We both know what I mean. Pick her up at the station, will you?'

I hung up and waited beside Judith on the grey platform. The other passengers gave us sidelong glances but did not come near. When the train approached I gripped her so tightly by the elbow that she flinched. I allowed myself a smile because I had been the cause of pain.

The train stopped. It was almost empty. I opened a door and guided Judith up the steps, then led her into a carriage. There were vacant seats just inside the sliding door. I pushed her into one. She sat down with her legs awry, her wrists crossed in her lap and her eyes fixed on the far end of the carriage.

'Alex will meet you,' I said, and left her there. I stepped off the train and slammed the door behind me just as it was about to pull away.

I had promised myself that I would not turn to look, but I did.

Judith was sitting in the position I had left her in, still staring ahead unseeingly. As the carriage rolled past she gave no indication that she could see me on the platform, and her face was free of all emotion. She might have been a statue, sculpted by a master, brought to life by a wizard, then deserted.

I closed the door behind me. Lillian was waiting in the kitchen. For as long as I had known her she had always been elegant; now her posture was graceless, almost ungainly.

'I did what we agreed,' I announced. 'It's over.'

She breathed out as if bonds had been eased.

'Judith Ford never meant much to me,' I continued. 'I never thought of leaving you or anything like that. I never wanted to. The idea didn't even cross my mind.'

I waited but she said nothing. Panic pressed its thin fingers against my ribcage. I needed to be certain that my life was still secure, even if it meant capitulating to Lillian's belief in my naïvety.

'You said I was foolish. I've been worse than that. Stupid would have been a better word. Idiotic, even.'

She nodded with a stiff-necked awkwardness. 'You're sure it's over between you? Tell me honestly.'

'Certain. Over forever.'

'You have to forget her.'

'I know.'

'It's easy for me; I never met the woman.'

'I'm pleased.'

'No, you don't understand. All she is to me is a kind of idea. Because I can't picture her she doesn't really exist as a person. I just think of her as—' The hesitation was only momentary. 'A mistress.'

Lillian walked across the room. She was still wearing outdoor shoes; the heels struck the floor-tiles like knuckles on a wooden door.

'We shouldn't really think of people like that. No one is ever just a mistress, like no one is ever just a mother or a daughter. But that's how I want to think of Judith Ford, Jamie. As a kind of object. I don't ever want to know anything about her as a person. I couldn't bear it.'

'I understand. I'll forget her easily. I promise I will.'

She walked back across the room and stood in front of me. 'We have to put all this behind us,' she insisted. 'We're strong enough to get over it; we both are. When Claire arrives she mustn't suspect a thing. Agreed?'

'Yes, agreed.'

Lillian reached up to the side of my head and ran her fingers through the hair above my left ear in a grooming motion. I moved my head like an animal eager to be pampered.

'If you want to tell me anything else,' she said, 'you'd better tell me now.'

I was instantly alert and suspicious. Lillian might know something she was keeping secret.

'You flinched,' she said.

'You caught a hair. It made me jump. No, there's nothing else I should tell you.'

'Did you hate saying goodbye?'

'Exactly the opposite.'

'Truly?'

'I swear it. Once Judith Ford had done her work on the estate I drove her to the station and left her on the platform. I don't expect to see her ever again.'

'Are you sure about that?'

I thought of Angie, operating a cash register in a city cafe, unrecognised by me until the last moment.

'She'll not see me if I see her first,' I answered firmly.

I believed I was telling the truth, but even as I spoke a sense of loss rang through me in a sad, extended note, like a welcoming horn calling for miles across a calm and shipless sea.

'Let's not talk any more about it,' I said. 'We have Claire's holiday to arrange. All right?'

'Yes,' she said, 'I agree.'

'We always enjoyed doing things together as a family. We don't get much chance now, and the chances lessen with each year that passes. So let's think out some ideas.'

'Right,' she said.

Lillian and I spent some time discussing possibilities.

After a while we decided that we could all go to a certain exhibition, a particular play, and possibly visit a nearby stately home. Providing Claire agreed, of course. Her flight was due in two days' time; when she arrived we would discuss our suggestions and draw up a plan. Whatever happened, we would be together as a family.

'It'll be like old times,' Lillian said.

'Yes,' I agreed, and began to think about Judith again.

At this very moment she would be with Alex. They would be huddled together, shipwrecked by failure, brooding over the sinking of their dreams.

'What are you thinking of?'

'What?'

'You've gone very quiet. What's on your mind?'

'I was thinking of Claire.'

Lillian took my hands again. She had feared that we would separate, and now she reassured herself by constantly touching me. 'You miss her, don't you?'

'Yes. More than I thought I ever would. She's always been really important to me. I love her as if she were our own daughter.'

'She *is* our own daughter.'

'You know what I mean. It doesn't make any difference to me that she's adopted.'

'It doesn't make any difference to any of us. It never has.'

'Did she ever—' And I stopped.

'Ever what?'

'Did she ever ask you about her real parents?'

Lillian shrugged. 'She knows their names; you know she does. But she's never talked to me about finding them. Is that what you mean?'

'I suppose so. Yes.'

'I don't think she thinks about them much. She got beyond that stage when she was fourteen.'

'Do you think she will? Ever want to find them?'

'If she wants to track them down there are organisations that can help her. But she's secure and she's happy. To be honest, I don't think her biological parents mean anything to her. We're her *real* parents.'

'You're right,' I said.

But I was thinking of a baby in a carrycot, her dead mother sprawled in the bedroom, and a young man hesitating on the landing outside.

Perhaps Grace had found real parents, too – parents mature enough to have let her live a happy childhood. Perhaps even now she was shaping a bright future.

It was even possible that we might pass by each other in the street and not recognise who we were or what we had been.

An hour later, when Lillian was taking a shower, the telephone rang.

'Jamie McGoldrick?'

I recognised the voice and for a brief moment wanted to cut the connection and leave the phone off the hook. But that would have been no good. Sooner or later he would ring again. And Lillian might answer.

'Where's Judith?'

'What do you mean? Didn't you meet her?'

'I waited for three trains. She wasn't on any of them. Then I came back here to the house to see if we'd somehow missed each other. There's no sign of her. Where is she?'

My chest felt hollow. 'I put her on the train and watched it pull out of the station. I don't know what's happened to her. She must have got off before she reached the end of the line.'

'Why would she do that?'

'I don't know.'

'What have you done to her?' There was menace in his voice.

'Nothing.'

'What did you tell her? What happened between the two of you?'

'Just the truth.'

'The truth? What truth?'

'The truth that she's not my daughter.'

There was silence at the other end.

'The truth that you're trying to defraud me, blackmail me.'

My voice shook as I finished the sentence. At first I did not recognise the emotion as self-pity.

'Jesus,' Alex said.

'She was shocked that I'd found out,' I went on, but my confidence was unexpectedly thin. 'She'll turn up. She'll be licking her wounds somewhere. Maybe she's frightened to tell you – have you considered that? I suspect that you're a violent man, Alex. Judith won't want you to take it out on her. She's maybe had enough of that in her life.'

'I've never touched her.'

I made no comment.

'Except once,' he said. 'We fought each other. From the Fords onwards, men have taken advantage of Judith. I never have. I've told you that already. I was speaking the truth. I always speak the truth.'

'The Fords? Her father?'

'He was a violent man. Why do you think she never went back?'

I could not answer.

'Are you telling *me* the truth, Jamie?'

'Yes.'

A pause. 'Swear that you are.'

'For God's sake—'

'Swear it.'

'Don't be so bloody Mediterranean.'

'On your mother's grave.'

'For God's sake, all right, if it will keep you quiet. I'm telling you the truth. I swear it.'

'On your mother's—'

'On my mother's grave, if you want me to.'

'Bastard,' he said.

The line went dead. I replaced the receiver.

After a few seconds I walked stealthily to the bathroom door. The shower was still hissing. Lillian would not have heard a thing.

Unseasonably heavy rain was falling by the time we reached the airport. I drove up the entrance ramp, stopped by one of the numbered pillars, and told Lillian I would meet her at Arrivals. She protested that she would prefer to stay with me. I reasoned that I might have to leave the car in the open and that there was little sense in us both getting wet.

The multi-storey park was nearly full but there were still some vacant spaces tucked half-hidden in the congested rows. I ignored them all and ascended the ramps until I reached the last, open level. It was almost empty. When I got out of the car I could see nothing but dull concrete parking bays made shiny by rain and a cold, low cloud which rumbled with aircraft noise.

I took the lift down to the concourse and made for the nearest rank of public telephones. Hunch-shouldered figures pale with travel stood at each one. I waited impatiently, unable to stand still, all the time watching the overhead arrival screens and listening to the metallic echoes of the public announcements.

By the time a phone became available the green numbers of Claire's flight were pulsing. Her plane had landed. My daughter was back in her home country again.

I did not have to wait long for Alex to answer. The ringing tone burred only twice before there was a fumbled click and a voice raised in brittle expectation.

'It's Jamie McGoldrick,' I said.

Silence. I could sense the collapse of hope.

'Are you all right?'

'I thought it was her,' he said.

Again and again over the last two days I had repeated a mantra – Judith Ford had nothing to do with me; she was not my daughter; she was an impostor and a charlatan. But I still felt an interior lurch of panic.

'There's still no sign?' I asked.

'There's been a sign all right.'

'What's happened?'

'I was at a gallery; you might know it.'

'The Tetmajer?'

'You know about it?'

'The new traditionalists? Yes.'

Perhaps realising the extent of my influence, Alex took stock before he spoke again.

'When I came back Judith had been in the house. She'd packed her things and gone.'

'Gone? Where to?'

'No one knows. A neighbour says she arrived just after I left, so she must have been watching, waiting for me to go. Half an hour later she left in a cab. She even put her keys through the front door, as if she no longer has a use for them.' He stopped talking for several seconds before he continued. 'This is all your fault.'

'At least you know she's safe and well.'

'I don't know that at all. Do you? The way you treated her she could be dead by now. She could have followed the example of her mother. That wouldn't surprise you, would it? She has a history of failed attempts. This time she might have succeeded.'

'I wanted to know that she was safe. You've told me that she is. That's all I want from you, Alex. I'm hanging up now.'

'She never even left a message. After all these years. The least I deserved was a note.'

'I have to go. I don't think we need speak to each other again.'

'She took your book. She left a lot of things that belong to her, but she took your book.'

'I'm going,' I said, and hung up.

I walked through the bright artificial spaces towards the arrivals lounge. Lillian was waiting for me there.

In a few minutes we would meet Claire again. We would embrace, perhaps shed a discreet tear, and like all people who truly love each other we might find words cumbersome after such a long separation. Within a short while everything would be fine. We would compete with stories of what had happened to us. Claire would tell us about America, Lillian would talk about England and friends. All I could do was mention the Peermain mound. The rest of what had happened would be kept secure, unmentioned, as tightly sealed as my past had been. I would carry my secrets with me to the grave.

The glass wall overlooking the runways was stippled with water. I could see the near edges of the dark aprons of concrete, but that was all. Everything else had vanished into rain and cloud. Our world had contracted to an area of brightly-lit comfort, where men and women came and went on journeys that were both mysterious and mundane, and where each one never really knew the other.

Somewhere out there, beyond the rain, the woman who was my real daughter was living her unseen, undetected life. So, too, was the woman who had come to me, claiming to be her.

I no longer knew if they were separate persons or the same.

7

By the time I arrived the gallery was already thronged with guests. I threaded my way through them with a price leaflet in one hand. Like analysts discussing the most profitable distribution of investment, they bandied talk of a new generation of Wyeths, Hockneys, Freuds, Pearlsteins. Unreal optimism pulsed through their conversations like a drug exciting a bloodstream.

At one side of the room Alex was talking animatedly to new disciples whose upper bodies were angled towards him. Our eyes met briefly and then he looked away. I knew he had been expecting me, because he was careful not to show any change in emotion.

I ignored the other hangings and edged my way to Alex's section of the exhibition. Small, inturned gatherings of people with wineglasses, cigarettes and assertive voices were ranged in front of the paintings like a breached barrier.

All of Alex's works were figurative. Idiosyncratically, the gallery had grouped them on either side of his publicity photograph, which was fixed to the wall as if it were part of the display. The photograph was a full-face portrait in high contrast and was faintly threatening. I studied the group of paintings to its left, but lingered on none.

Here was the artist's dead father, his head thrown back

on sunlit and bloody flagstones, a stiffened expression of surprise on his face. Here was Alex himself, pictured as a sullen genius with muddied paint daubing his hands. Here were a father and daughter, seated side by side like monarchs, but with the man reaching across to touch his pubescent child on her breasts. And here, too, was my own face, as monumental as a sculpture, looking guiltily out of a frame whose sides crowded me like the walls of a prison cell.

I heard my name spoken and turned to find Edgar Tetmajer standing beside me. We shook hands and he began to talk quickly. He asked after Lillian, and then my daughter – Claire, was it? I told him they were both fine, and that Claire had recently returned to the States after a short visit home. He nodded and told me about his own sons, as if fatherhood somehow made us comrades. Then, formalities over, he turned to the exhibition.

He was grateful for my attendance; grateful, too, for my suggestion that he acquaint himself with the work of Alexandros Stylianou. Much interest had already been expressed in this painter – and, indeed, all the other exhibitors.

'I can't stay long,' I explained. 'I have my own project to oversee.'

'On the old Peermain estate? It's progressing well?'

'The site's being cleared today. Part of my chosen area is being tested by surveyors. I should be there.'

'I understand. Are they checking if buttressing will be needed?'

'Yes. Don't ask me any more, Edgar. You know I'll not tell you.'

'Of course,' he said, looking slyly at Alex's portrait of me. 'But you can tell me your reactions to this.'

'Not many subjects feel flattered by their portraits these days.'

'They are merely subjects. You're a professional. You can understand the structure, the balances, the choices that an artist makes. Look at the restricted framing of the image. Do you think that young Stylianou has seen into a part of you that no one else has reached?'

'I think he may imagine that he does. That doesn't mean that he has.'

'Perhaps in the future you'll not think that.'

'No, I don't think I'll alter my opinion.'

'I expect that our Cypriot friend is about to become very famous, Jamie. Two profiles of him are being written already. Did you know the dead man in that painting is his murdered father? There's a photograph of the crime; Alex has it on the wall of his house. But perhaps you've already seen it?'

'No, I don't think I have.'

'It's very dramatic. I imagine that picture editors are negotiating reprint rights at this very moment. They like that sort of thing. And this seated couple, here, are people he saw on a train. It would be a disturbing piece anyway, but have you read the title? *Father and Daughter*. Very strange.'

'Yes. Very.'

'Alex told me that he was fascinated by the way in which the man tormented his child. He didn't treat her like a daughter at all, but like a plaything he was both charmed and repelled by. Extraordinary, don't you think? The man despised the girl and yet he was besotted by her. He's exercising a crude power over her. But perhaps, in her turn, she too is exercising a kind of control.'

'You may be right. Who knows?'

Edgar leaned closer to me. 'If you wish to make an investment, Jamie, it would be wise to buy one of Stylianou's works. I believe we will have sold most of them very soon. And before long his asking prices will have to be increased.'

'I'll think about it.'

'And have you seen the studies of his favourite model? He had dozens, perhaps hundreds to show me. I chose a mere handful.'

We moved to the next section of the display, on the right of Alex's photograph. Edgar raised a hand and gently eased aside a small group of guests who were standing too close to the display.

Images of Judith had been hung next to each other as if in an iconostasis. Her face stared at me from each canvas.

In the first painting she sat reflectively in an armchair, hugging to her chest a closed book with a shiny cover. I wondered if it had been mine.

In the next she stood in contemplative part-profile like a model in a blue-period Picasso; in another, she ran flexed fingers through damp-darkened hair while drops of water shone on the side of her neck. Still further right, and partly obscured by a guest with a walking-stick who stood chatting to two women companions, I saw that Alex had, after all, painted Judith naked.

She was sitting in the same chair that she had sat in with the book, a chair I now recognised as the one in the front room of Alex's house. Her bare legs were drawn up in front of her body and her arms were pressed together so that the fists rested under her chin, screening her breasts. It was a position both enticing and demure.

'Do you like them?' Edgar asked.

I felt a shudder of revulsion. Edgar was a businessman and an aesthete, but in that common, everyday phrase he had unexpectedly sounded like a pimp.

I was as noncommittal as I could be. 'They're okay.'

In return, he became more confidential.

'Between you and me, I'm not convinced that Stylianou has quite mastered the portrayal of individual character. Look at this girl. Do you know what I see?'

'I have no idea, Edgar.'

'I see you.'

I had half-expected the comparison, but there was still an inner lurch, a moment of vertigo, a drying of the mucus around the tongue.

'Don't you see it?' he asked.

I shook my head. I wanted to lean against something.

'Perhaps it's difficult if you yourself are a subject,' he mused. 'I have to confess that I noticed it immediately.'

'This woman has nothing to do with me,' I insisted.

He looked at me with surprise. 'Of course not. I didn't suggest that she had. I'm merely commenting on the artist's limitations; limitations which others cannot yet see.'

I followed Edgar as he moved a few paces to the right, his hand extended again. The man with the stick reluctantly shuffled even further out of the way and we stood before Alex's last painting.

'A curious work,' Edgar commented, 'quite unlike his others. It has an enigmatic quality, don't you think – like late Gauguin. Notice the naked girl, the crib in the background, the man at the door. There's a suggestion that something is happening, but we don't know what. Have you read the title? *The Game Of The Few*? Alex didn't tell me what that meant. I'm sure it's a quotation; I've seen it somewhere else. But I don't recognise the author.'

I had to lick my lips before I could speak. 'Berkeley,' I told him.

'Really? And the relevance?'

I shook my head. He went on.

'He painted this very recently. Perhaps it heralds a change of direction.'

To me the large canvas was reminiscent of the dreamy menace of Delvaux or the eroticised mannequins of Balthus. In a dusky room a naked woman lay on an unmade bed, hands by her sides, eyes staring at the ceiling. Her flesh was unblemished but at the far limit of ripeness, like a fruit about to be bruised. Beneath her body the furled white sheets suggested an unwrapped shroud. Beyond the bed, opening to either side of the very meridian of the image, were two doors. Behind one was a cot with a child. Behind the other, a man stood on a landing with a stair-rail curving away behind him into darkness. I looked closely at the figure. Its features were unrecognisable.

'It's the same female model, of course,' Edgar continued. 'That's why we placed it at the end of this group. I asked Alex if the composition represents something that has actually happened. He told me he'd imagined it.'

He paused, as if he had only just realised that Alex's answer had been ambiguous rather than clear. Then he continued.

'You'll notice how the solitary nude is isolated still further by the diagrammatic nature of the composition. At first I thought the woman was selling herself, that she needed the man's custom, his money. After all, it appears that she has a child. So at first I read the picture as valid, but unoriginal, social commentary. Now I've begun to think that the woman is dead.'

'You think so?'

'If you compare her posture to the posture of the artist's murdered father you will see that they are extraordinarily similar. So yes, I believe she's dead. But I don't know how that alters the relationships within this canvas. What do you think?'

'I do my best not to read meanings into art.'

'Perhaps you're wise, Jamie. After all, the artist himself is saying nothing. A gambit he learned from you, perhaps?'

'I have to go. I'm expected at the estate. I have an appointment with the company representative.'

I did not tell Edgar, but I was also due to meet Terry Evans.

Letting him see the cleared site, before my own work began, was both a small demonstration of gratitude and, perhaps, a way of blunting any future criticism he might make about the reshaping of the land.

'Again, thank you for coming,' Edgar said. 'Can I not persuade you to make an investment? Perhaps I could even trim the price a little; who knows?'

'I'm tempted by this one,' I said, nodding at *The Game Of The Few*.

He touched my arm like a practised haggler. 'If you like it so much, I can promise to let you have first refusal.'

I glanced at the price list which was still in my hand.

'You're asking too much, Edgar. I think you should come down a little. After all, I was the one who put you in touch with Alex Stylianou. And if I wanted to, I'd be able to buy work from him privately, without going through the Tetmajer. This one just takes my fancy, that's all.'

Edgar pretended to be thoughtful, but I realised this was merely one of his negotiating ruses. 'I did imply we'd be able to shave the price a little,' he admitted.

'I really must go,' I said. 'I'll contact you tomorrow. We'll see if we can reach an agreement.'

'I can ring you.'

'No,' I said quickly, 'I'll ring *you*.'

He nodded understandingly. 'Of course,' he said. 'A gift, perhaps for your wife. One has to be discreet.'

'Well, maybe you're right,' I said, and then shook his hand and walked away.

As I made my way to the exit I waited for my name to be called. I was certain Alex would not remain among his admirers and let me leave.

'Mr McGoldrick.'

There were two clear yards of polished floorboard between myself and the door. I stopped and turned.

Alex had broken away. He had pursued me through the critics and the artists and the lecturers and the socialites, and now he stood in front of me, a little thinner than before, his face sharper, his hair more artfully dishevelled, his fingers turpentined free of stains. An almost-empty wineglass was held awkwardly in one hand, as if he was not sure what to do with it.

'Why did you come here?' he asked.

'Duty.'

'To her?'

I folded the price list and threw it back onto the table I had picked it up from. 'To Edgar Tetmajer.'

'You've heard nothing?'

'Have you?'

He shook his head. Just like the Peermain claimant, Judith had vanished back into her own past.

'I thought she would have got in touch,' I lied. 'In fact, I thought she would go back to you.'

Loss tugged at his words. 'I don't know where she is. I don't know what she's doing. She's walked out of my life completely.'

'I see.'

'She might even be dead.'

I answered with flimsy confidence. 'You've said that before.'

'Yes. But now I believe it might be true.'

'I don't think so. Judith's too tough to give in.'

'She didn't change you. You learned nothing. You still don't recognise fragility when you see it.'

I took a step nearer to the door.

'You broke her like a man crushes an eggshell, Jamie. You turned your back on her twice. Once was cruelty enough, but a second time . . .'

I turned away and pushed open the door but did not hold it. As it swung behind me I heard the thump of his palm hitting the wood. He was only two steps behind. We passed quickly through the reception area and approached the glass outer doors which led onto the busy street.

'You didn't tell me why you came,' he said angrily.

'I've given you an answer.'

'You lied. You didn't come here for Edgar Tetmajer.'

I stepped out into the heat and the downfall sunlight and began to walk along the pavement. Alex followed me, raising his voice so that he could be heard above the traffic noise.

'You came here for Judith,' he said accusingly.

I stopped and faced him. There was no alternative. His mouth was slightly open. He was so excited that the bright pink tip of his tongue could be seen between his teeth. He had been too preoccupied to rid himself of his glass so, absurdly, he was still holding it in one hand. A tiny amount of red wine, made pale by the light, trembled above its shining stem.

'Take my advice, Alex – forget her.'

'I can't. Neither can you.'

'She's part of the past. For both of us. Pick some other model; lavish your talent on her.' Despite myself, I could not help but give a slight downturn to my pronunciation of *talent*.

'She's your daughter. How can you give me such advice?'

'It's time to widen your range. And keep away from imaginative reconstructions of suicide. You put Judith at the centre of that image. You had no right. You're using someone else's tragedy to further your own career.'

Alex shook his head angrily. 'I have the same rights as every other artist. The same as you. All I do is follow precedents that were set hundreds of years ago. A painter must deal with suffering or he is nothing. I've used my own past. Why shouldn't I use the past of the woman who shared my life?'

Traffic drummed along the road. The air was congested with the smell of dust and petrol.

'I always thought that I was good,' he admitted. 'Now, with *The Game Of The Few*, I know that I'm exceptional. It's my best work. That was evident even to you, Jamie. I watched you study that canvas. You recognised a new quality as soon as you saw it.'

I nodded reluctantly. He went on.

'I thought you would resent the painting, but while you were talking to Edgar Tetmajer he gave me a sly, tiny sign – a thumbs up. I thought he was telling me you had bought it. Have you?'

'No. I'm still thinking about it.'

'Why should you want it?'

I said nothing. His face tightened.

'You want to destroy it,' he said.

I looked away.

'It's my best work, a new beginning, and you want to buy it in order to burn it. What kind of artist are you? What kind of father?'

I faced Alex again.

'What kind? The kind who's more successful than you could ever be. I'm a contented man, Alex. Not many people in this world can claim that. I've worked my way up from nothing and now I have the kind of life that you must envy. Maybe that's why you and Judith tried to destroy it. Maybe that's why you're still trying. I hate your painting. It exploits me and slanders my past. It may be an advance for you, it may be technically superior to your other work, but it's meretricious.'

'You're trying to justify destruction. That can't be defended.'

'Believe me, I could defend it. I have enough experience to make a watertight case.'

'I could paint another. Easily. I put my subjects through many variations. You've said so yourself.'

'Correct. But you won't, because you owe me everything. I recommended your work to Edgar Tetmajer. That's why he came to see you. Your success is due entirely to me. I've given you what you always wanted. In a way, you've won. One of the reasons Judith and you hatched your scheme was to get my support, my patronage.'

'That's not true. I didn't need you to get me this exhibition. I would have got started without you. Or Edgar Tetmajer. It might have taken a little more time, that's all.'

'And it might never have happened. Sometimes there's no correlation between artistic worth and recognition. We both know that's true.'

As if his skin were absorbing the force of my gaze he looked down self-consciously at the pale wine for a few seconds. Then he walked across to a yellow refuse container fixed on the side of a lamp-post and dropped the glass into it. Despite the noise of passing cars I still heard the faint click as it fell onto something metallic.

I followed him like a hunter refusing escape to his prey. 'Now that Judith has gone,' I said, 'you and I have to reach an agreement.'

'You want to buy my silence.'

'I think I've already bought it. Don't you?'

'And my painting? *The Game Of The Few*?'

'I'm not going to destroy your painting. I'm going to buy it and hide it away from the world. No one is going to see it. In return, you'll do no more like it. Or any further images of me. You'll deny any relationship between Judith Ford and myself. You'll swear, just like you made me swear, that we had nothing to do with each other.'

Alex looked up and down the street as if invaders from the past could appear at any moment.

'I take it you've told no one of your real source for that painting,' I said.

'No,' he confessed, 'I've said nothing about your past. I don't intend to. If you want an agreement, you have it.'

'Swear it.'

'On my father's grave.'

I felt myself relax. 'Good,' I said.

'I'm not doing it for you. I'm doing it for Judith.'

I shook my head uncomprehendingly.

'I have to hope that she's still alive,' Alex said, his voice brittle. 'I must believe that someday she'll come back. Suppose she returned and found that I'd made her secret known to the world? Could you predict how she'd react? I couldn't; I have no idea. But she might turn on her heel and walk away forever. I can't take that chance.'

'My God,' I said, 'you really do love her.'

'It was foolish of me to become so involved. I'm an artist. That's the meaning and purpose of my life. Anything else is secondary and expendable. The thing you call love is an indulgence and a threat. Neither you nor I should have succumbed to it.'

'But we did?'

'I fell. Just once. You fell twice. It's plain to anyone what you feel for Lillian. You must ask yourself whether her effect on your work has been good or bad. But you loved Judith as well, as only a father could love his daughter. And she loved you.'

'That's not true.'

'Only people who love each other could be as cruel as you have been. If Judith had not loved you, do you think she would have stayed away?'

I was dizzy. The heat, I thought; I must get in out of the sunlight.

'She lied to me, Alex. You both did.'

'A little. We didn't tell you the truth about what happened when we found out who you were. I admit that.'

'The truth is that you decided to take me for what you could get. You constructed a story you were certain I would fall for. It was successful for a while. But I found out. Eventually, I found out.'

He looked at me for several seconds before he spoke again. Time dilated around us. Even the passing cars moved as if in a film run slowly.

'The truth is I begged her to leave you alone,' he said at last.

'Liar,' I said. I did not hesitate before using the word. And then, abruptly and without warning, I was scared.

Perhaps a great truth had been offered to me, but I had refused to recognise it and now it was being taken away. Months ago, when Judith had threatened to cut short our first conversation, I had been unmanned by the same irrational fear. I had always trusted myself to create a coherent world from the apparently random acts, stories, and landscapes that excited and intrigued me. Perhaps this time I had created a false world, a chimera, made not from insight but from a kind of corruption.

'Don't believe me, then,' Alex answered bitterly. 'I'll tell you nothing else.'

'No,' I said, 'go on.'

He stared down the road.

'Please,' I added.

'We argued.'

'And?'

'I didn't want Judith to do it. She forced the issue; she wouldn't bend. Things were said that I'll never forget. She tried to hit me, kick me. I had to defend myself. We were each covered in bruises. They were still there the first time that you met. She said that she wanted to be dressed smartly to meet you. She chose a long skirt to cover them. It was the only time we fought, and we vowed never to fight again.'

'Go on.'

'I told her how risky it was. I said how you might not want to know her, how you might think she was an impostor.

I even thought you could be an evil person, vindictive enough to ruin my career. That's why she didn't tell you that I'm a painter; not until later.'

'She wanted help for you. She was open about that.'

'I told you she was honest. Too honest to accept a bribe. That's why she tore up your cheque.'

I said nothing. My mouth was as dry as the sand I had buried in the glacier.

'Maybe she realised that you'd turn on her. Perhaps she wanted something tangible for me before your relationship broke apart. I never asked for help. From the very beginning, I didn't want her to contact you. I wanted things to stay as they were between us.'

'But I had nothing to do with the life you lived together. I couldn't have affected it.'

'She goes from man to man. Don't you realise that? I thought I'd rescued her. I thought she'd changed, that she was happy with me. And she was.'

'So?'

'I was only a lover. You're her father. I was nothing compared to you.'

I shook my head.

His eyes were as dark as his past.

'Don't fool yourself, Jamie,' he said. 'You're her father. In all kinds of ways. You have to live with that. You may have rejected her twice, but you'll never be cured of her infection. On the day that you die, you'll still be thinking of her.'

I began to walk along the pavement, away from him.

'On the day that I die I'll be thinking of my own life, and Lillian's, and Claire's, and most of all I'll be thinking of my work. You'll have been long forgotten. Both of you.'

This time Alex did not attempt to follow. 'You may forget me,' he said, 'but you'll never forget Judith. You were never able to forget her. You and I are alike, Jamie. We're both prisoners of our past.'

I had no more to say to him, and I did not want to hear whatever else he might say to me.

I walked away as quickly as I could, keeping my head down, pushing aside people who got in my way.

When I reached the car I cast a furtive glance behind me, but I had not been pursued. I was bitter and angry. Alex Stylianou would be back inside the gallery by now, frittering away his time with those who had no sense of innovation, lapping up their praise like a dog laps up vomit.

I drove away trying to pretend that there was nothing else for me to worry about. Like a good accountant, I had balanced the ledgers and drawn a line under the result. But I was fooling myself. I knew I could never rest, and all the way to the estate I was haunted by the memory of my lost daughter.

For more than half my life Grace had been at the edge of my awareness, and for much of that time she had fastened into my conscience like a parasite hooked into its host. I had known her only as a baby, but my memories of her were detailed and immediate. No matter how desperately I tried, I had never been able to efface them.

And I had never been able to imagine Grace as an adult, except as a facsimile of Eve. I had not even been able to visualise the clothes she might wear. In my mind she dressed like her mother's revenant, in the outmoded styles of an ageing generation. Despite the many years I had spent brooding about her, Grace remained a numinous figure. And because I had never been able to fully imagine her, she had never truly existed for me. She was a theory, a concept, a function, as lifeless as a mannequin in a philosopher's proposition.

But now my daughter had ceased to belong to an irrecoverable and unwanted past. She had walked out of it and into the present like a spirit stepping through a mirror. She had returned with a face, a figure, a history, a new name. She had stood beside me, taken my hand, murmured her confidences, insinuated herself into my dreams.

And who was she? Someone moulded by the blind compulsions of genetics. A woman whose obsessions and failures reflected and distorted both her mother's and my own. I had thought that I was travelling an untroubled road, but the darkness and rubble of Judith's life had made it as unpredictable as a labyrinth.

I followed the Peermain driveway automatically, not even glancing across the parkland to the wood, and reversed the car into a free space next to Terry Evans's car. Before leaving I pulled down the visor above the windscreen. It had a mirror on its underside, and by turning it at an angle I could study my own face.

I did not have to look for long. Judith Ford stared out at me from my own reflection.

I went to the reception area and said that Ken Takama was expecting me. The receptionist was new; I had never met her before. She told me that Mr Takama had left a few minutes ago with his other visitor. Although her voice was neutral her face was slightly flustered.

'They'll be at the mound,' I said. 'I'll meet them there.'

'I've been advised that no one else should go to the mound, sir.'

I laughed. 'It's all right. I designed the new one. I'm the man in charge.'

I went back outside. Before walking across the park I paused beside the first Interlocking Piece and touched the surface like a believer caressing a reliquary.

When I was a child I had spent weeks playing with the progenitor of the Interlocking Pieces. It was a simple toy, bought at some faraway novelty shop, comprising eight elements which slid and clicked together in sequence to form a three-dimensional star with a dozen points. The puzzle was stabilised by the satisfying insertion, often deliberately delayed by me, of one final, smoothly-turned element which locked all the pieces into place. Even then the star's capacity to give simple pleasure was not exhausted. It could be rolled along the ground, and even lobbed into the air and caught, without breaking apart. Until one day when my father, in a bottomless rage of frustration at being shackled by his own life, scooped up the scattered pieces and threw them onto a smouldering fire. I rescued every piece but one, and that was the locking piece.

I lifted my hand and looked down the long sweep of parkland. Fragments of bark were strewn like scraps of paper across grass which was stamped with the repeated geometries of machinery tracks. I had not realised that logging equipment would mark the land so easily. At the edge of the wood, to one side of the next Interlocking Piece, a Land Rover and a car were parked. The car must have been driven too quickly, for the ground was torn into long muddy scythes where the tyres had slid.

Everything was quiet as I walked towards the wood. I expected to hear the chug of motors or the dental whine of chainsaws; instead there was nothing but the soft noise of my own footfalls. It must have been as quiet as this when the Peermains had taken up their poses for Gainsborough.

The Land Rover belonged to the surveyors; I could see some of their equipment still inside. The car had the jacket of a suit bundled carelessly onto the back seat. In its lapel was an identity badge with Ken Takama's name on it. I tested the car door. It had been left open.

Shards of muddy light glittered mysteriously among the shorn blades of grass. I walked over and bent to examine them. They came from Judith's twin mirror. The glass had been stepped on, driven over, shattered.

I straightened up, crossed a few more yards of space, and entered the wood.

Heavy machinery had churned the soil. The undergrowth was flattened and snapped branches hung limply from rhododendron bushes. Crimson petals were spilled on the ground beneath them.

White marker tape was still attached to the tree-trunks, but it had been severed between them. The trailing ends lay trampled underfoot. Beyond the tape there had been nothing but greenery and shadow, but now that the trees were felled a great chasm of sunlight illuminated the centre of the wood. The shape of the mound was clearly visible. Dust hung in the air, trapping the smells of earth, combustion, crushed greenery, bleeding sap.

I crossed the torn barrier and entered a raw clearing. Hundreds of flying insects rose and fell in the sunlight. Facing me was a silent machine with a scratched yellow body and a bright steel claw raised motionless in the air. Stripped tree-trunks lay around it like vanquished enemies. The cab door hung open; there was no driver.

I stepped across sheaves of lopped branches and approached the base of the mound. Men in overalls and safety helmets were gathered around a metal ladder which leaned against the side as if it were being used to break a siege.

Ken Takama stood among the men, his arms folded so that his white shirt was tightly stretched across his muscular back. Sweat marked it in wide patches, and his shoes and trousers were coated with soil. One foot was still on the lowest rung of the ladder, as if he had just descended from the summit.

Nothing was happening. No one moved. The entire area was quiet except for the buzz of insects.

'Is something wrong?' I asked. I took care to speak in a hushed voice but it was still too loud, like a shout at a funeral.

The men turned towards me. Nothing was said. Ken took his foot from the ladder and glanced towards its upper rungs. No one else was coming down it.

'What's going on?' I asked, looking at the shifty, puzzled

faces. None of them met my eyes. They were like men quietened by shame.

'Terry Evans is up there,' Ken said. 'Everyone else has come down. It was for the best, Jamie. The police will be here soon.'

'Police?'

For a moment I wondered what the police had to do with this bizarre little congregation. Then I felt a sensation like a knife being drawn down my spine. My God, I thought, they've found Judith.

I grasped the sides of the ladder and put my foot on the lowest rung. The metal was hot to the touch.

'I'm going up,' I said hoarsely, and began to climb. The hollow frame clanged with noises like a line of cell doors being closed.

'Jamie, we have to stop everything,' Ken said urgently. 'It could take days, weeks.'

I ignored him. From the direction of the church the blare of a police siren began to saw rhythmically through the quiet.

I was holding my breath as the top of the mound came into view. There was only one person there, and that was Terry Evans. There was nothing suspicious at all – no clothing, no shoes, no suicide's corpse. Instead a country vicar knelt at the centre of the depression, his sandy hair disarranged, his hands pressed together as if he were about to bless the site.

I breathed out again. Whatever the problem was, it was less dramatic, less personal than I had feared. I began to think that some kind of treasure had been found – a thief's hoard, perhaps, or a cache of silver from the eighteenth century.

The summit had been partly excavated, partly trampled. The dandelions and daisies were crushed and clods of upturned soil were strewn everywhere. Several probes had been thrust into the heart of the mound, leaving neat bullet-like holes, and two boxes of electronic sensors gleamed metallically where they had been apparently abandoned. A core sampler straddled the far rim, and two spades stood beside it like markers. There a faint gaseous smell, as if traces of methane were seeping from the vandalised ground.

The upturned soil had dried in the heat. Scattered amongst it were a few thin white sticks. They were slightly curved, like parts of a shattered hoop. I was sure I knew what they were. When I had last talked to Terry Evans I had imagined a celebration at the mound's completion. These fragile remains were the stems of clay pipes, snapped and cast aside by their owners more than two hundred years ago.

'Terry?' I asked.

He looked up at me. His face was heavy with shock. 'I didn't believe it when they told us,' he said.

'Told you what?'

He looked down again. I saw that his hands were clenched together.

'About this,' he said.

'You uncovered these?'

He shook his head rapidly. 'Of course not. I've touched nothing. The spades have done enough damage.'

I noticed even more white sticks protruding from the ransacked soil. A few feet away, at the further edge of the depression, the surveyors had partly uncovered a small, flat, pale stone. Two near-perfect circles of black earth were set within it, like eerie negatives of Judith's mirrors reflecting the sky.

Still puzzled, I studied the wreckage. I began to detect a suggestion of order, of pattern. Even the geometries of the exposed stone suggested a function or a purpose.

I dropped to my knees opposite Terry and picked up the

nearest fragment of stick. It was astonishingly white and seemed to have no weight at all.

'It looks like a piece of rib,' I said.

Terry waited for a disbelieving second before he answered.

'That's right,' he said; 'a child's rib.'

Suddenly I realised what I was looking at. Understanding broke through me and flooded my imagination. My hand began to tremble.

I gently replaced the rib among the wilderness of bones and stared beyond them. What I had thought was an oddly-shaped stone was a tiny half-uncovered skull. The earth-packed orbits stared upwards into the brilliant, unseen sunlight.

'The clothing must have rotted,' Terry went on, 'but the shoes were leather. They could still be on her feet. Beneath the surface, they could still be there.'

An anger to know the truth seized me. I reached forward and pushed the ends of my fingers into the soil between the ribs and the skull. Beneath the powdery grains I could feel a damp chill.

'Don't do it,' Terry said, 'you're disturbing the evidence.'

I heard the police car race across the parkland. The siren had been switched off but the tyres whirred and skidded on the grass.

I raked my fingers through the ground, opening a furrow several inches long. One of my nails tore. The deeper earth was black with moisture. I dug again. This time I felt an artificial shape, a hard smooth edge, beneath the tip of one finger.

'Leave it alone, Jamie,' Terry pleaded; 'you don't know what you're doing.'

I ignored him and scrabbled further. The edge belonged to something thin, metallic, wrought. It only took a few seconds to bring it to light and rub the soil from its surface.

A gold locket shone brightly in the sun. It was heart-shaped and attached to a thin chain whose links vanished beneath the earth.

Neither of us said anything for several seconds, and then Terry spoke.

'He did it,' he said.

The murdered child's locket shone out across the years that separated us.

Terry's eyes filled with tears. His voice began to crack under the weight of his emotion. 'He lied to everyone – the police, his wife. He even lied about the poor girl who shares their grave. She must have been a total stranger. He even let her be given his name. He knew it wasn't hers.'

'He must have thought it was necessary.'

'But all the time he knew where his real daughter was, and what he had done to her. What kind of a man must he have been, to do something like this? How could he have lived with his guilt? How could he have lied all his life?'

'But he got away with it,' I said.

'No,' Terry answered, 'he was punished. There's always a settling of accounts. God makes sure of that. Even if Archie Sproat didn't recognise it, he was still condemned.'

Strength flowed out of my limbs and disappeared into the soil like sacrificial blood.

I laid the gold locket back on the soil. I had had enough of uncertainty, enough of torment. I was eager for this part of my life to be over. I wanted to think of nothing but my own success.

I closed my eyes, raised my head to the sun, and imagined that everything had been solved – the murdered child buried, the mound clad in white reflective stone. I thought of sun striking the white dome and of the polished marble reflecting its pure brightness. I thought of all my other sculpture, distributed across the world in memorials that would stand for thousands of years, catching illumination as the earth turned, dimming as it plunged into darkness.

And suddenly, frighteningly, I thought of meltwater pouring from the collapsing end of a glacier, and of imprisoned sand moving unstoppably towards its cascade into the light.

It was going to happen much sooner than I had planned. Perhaps, I thought, it might even happen as early as next year.